# VAX HUMANA

# VAX HUMANA

## THE UNBELIEVABLE MR. BROWNSTONE™ BOOK THIRTEEN

MICHAEL ANDERLE

LMBPN Publishing
PMB 196, 2540 South Maryland Pkwy
Las Vegas, NV 89109

First US edition, November 2018
Version 1.03, January 2021

THE VAX HUMANA TEAM

**Special Thanks**
to Mike Ross
for BBQ Consulting
Jessie Rae's BBQ - Las Vegas, NV

**Thanks to the JIT Readers**

John Ashmore
Misty Roa
Keith Verret
Kelly O'Donnell
Nicole Emens
Daniel Weigert
James Caplan
Paul Westman
Angel LaVey
Danika Fedeli
Thomas Ogden
Larry Omans

*If I've missed anyone, please let me know!*

**Editor**
Lynne Stiegler

*To Family, Friends and*
*Those Who Love*
*to Read.*
*May We All Enjoy Grace*
*to Live the Life We Are*
*Called.*

# CHAPTER ONE

The woman relaxed in her red chaise lounge, the tension fading from her shoulders after a long day. The floor-to-ceiling windows provided a view of a stunning expanse of the ocean. Only a few clouds floated in the sky, and the bright sun illuminated the crystal-blue water below. A few white dots glided in the distance; gulls, she assumed.

*So much life on this planet.*

She smiled, taking a moment to appreciate the gorgeous sights. A few seconds later, she lifted her communicator and activated the feed to her ocular implants. Her smile vanished as the same message she'd been looking at the previous day appeared.

**Sentry 7921, Shepherd 2nd Class Aiyn Noraz Hal. Report received.**

**Command is evaluating all provided intelligence. All standing orders remain. Do not engage any non-Earth or non-Oriceran targets except in self-defense,**

**including suggested Vax Forerunner candidate identified in your report as the human James Brownstone.**

*He's not a human!*

**At this time, analysis suggests target confusion. Candidate behavior is well outside known Forerunner parameters. Based on low probability and potential magical explanation, no resources will or should be tasked at this time to engage target.**

**Repeat: All standing orders remain. Existing Concealment Protocol remains primary order.**

When Aiyn had first received the response weeks prior, she had thrown her communicator across the room so hard she'd cracked her window. Less sturdy glass and her communicator would have tumbled into the ocean below. While repair of her equipment was within reach, full fabrication of new advanced devices would require help from off-world. Protocol dictated a potential follow-up after loss of communication for a lengthy period, but the Alliance might take months to check on her in such a case.

Aiyn sighed. She wasn't sure why she continued to torture herself by reviewing the message, as if she thought it would change or they would inform her they'd been wrong and that reinforcements were on the way.

Each new report she'd sent from Earth had received only standard replies. Her few follow-up inquiries had been answered with nothing but "All standing orders remain." A monster walked on Earth, and her superiors only cared about her not exposing herself to humans and Oricerans.

What was the point of being a Shepherd if she ignored the monsters threatening her flock?

The truth was undeniable. Her superiors intended to do nothing despite a Forerunner preparing the battlefield for its comrades.

She had hoped that sending verbal reports instead of text messages would have communicated the gravity of the situation, but they didn't care. They'd sent her to Earth to watch for trouble but now acted as if she'd spotted an inconvenience distracting her from her real mission.

The damned Forerunner walked freely on the planet. A Vanguard would soon follow. Then the Destroyers would come, and the Vax would lay waste to Earth and Oriceran.

The Nine Systems Alliance could still prevent an invasion. All they had to do was stop Brownstone. Despite their holes in understanding the Vax, all available intelligence pointed to a successful defeat of a Forerunner forestalling an invasion. Permanently? Who could say, but at least then the world could be fortified.

*If we told the damned humans and Oricerans, they could probably figure out some way to stop the Vax gates with magic.*

No one understood fully what it meant or why the Vax didn't send the Destroyers first, but the pattern was undeniable. Aiyn didn't care if it was religious, strategic, or mere bravado—the invasion pattern was one of the few exploitable weaknesses they could use against the mysterious and deadly enemy.

Aiyn had held some small hope that magic would prove an effective counter against the Vax, but the encounter at the theme park had only reinforced the opposite conclusion. The symbiont could adapt to anything, even the strange magic of the creature calling itself "He Who Hunts." She snorted and deactivated the communicator before tossing it to the other side of her seat.

Could she be missing some brilliant strategy employed by her superiors? All right, mere visual records weren't concrete proof, but the probability of Brownstone's armor and weaponry coincidentally resembling Vax technology so closely was low even if he wasn't demonstrating the same level of destructive power yet. Brownstone behaving differently made perfect sense to her if he were adapting to local conditions, so she didn't understand why the analysts offered idiotic conclusions.

*It's a trick or a strategy. Even the Vax must realize that the scope of magic on Earth and Oriceran is so vast and different from what they are used to that their standard strategy might not be enough. It's obvious that Brownstone has been using his job as a bounty hunter to expose himself to different attacks and slowly build up his defenses. The theme park battle must have forced his hand, but he's still vulnerable. Otherwise, he would have initiated the next stage.*

*Even if the Forerunner is being stealthy, the Vanguard won't be.*

Aiyn took a deep breath and slowly let it out. She didn't have good information on Brownstone's adaptation range, so she could only assume it was already deep and vast. He'd been fighting both conventional and magical threats for years. He might be one of the most well-adapted Forerunners in the entire galaxy.

She couldn't remember a single case of a Forerunner spending years on a planet before initiating open attacks. Perhaps her superiors felt that proved there was no threat, but a continually adapting symbiont was a weapon slowly becoming undefeatable.

Few Vax invasions had been stopped by the time the Destroyers had arrived, unless they wanted to count bombarding and glassing an entire planet's surface. Several had been stopped by defeating the Vanguard.

No. They needed to stop the Forerunner, so they needed to take the present opportunity.

Her superiors wouldn't do anything. Thus, it fell on her.

Aiyn paced, her hands clenched into fists.

*Why did I join the Alliance Military? Why did I become a Shepherd? I knew I might never encounter a Vax, but I was supposed to be watching Earth for outside influences, and the damned Vax are certainly that.*

"No," she whispered, "not this time. Not this planet."

No reinforcements or supplies would be forthcoming, and if she went to the human authorities, she might only risk other trouble, not to mention earning the wrath of her superiors. Even if the self-sacrifice were worth it, an open attack against Brownstone using her full technology might speed up the invasion if she failed and he realized Alliance forces were on Earth.

Aiyn walked over to the window and placed a hand against the cool glass. "I'll give you what you expect, Brownstone, until it's too late, and then you'll die. You're nothing but a puppet of a biomechanical machine anyway. I'm doing you a favor. May the Spirits be kinder to you in your next life."

It was time to save the Earth.

A few hours later, Aiyn sat on the edge of her lush four-poster bed, a red robe clinging to her. Her human form was attractive by their standards, she supposed, even if it was still hard on her after many years to look in a mirror and not see blue skin and yellow eyes.

*This is the sacrifice of a Shepherd—to give ourselves up to save others.*

She ran her finger across a silver bracelet on her wrist, an AllBand computing device disguised as human jewelry. It always reminded her of the day her life changed. The day life had changed for many of her people.

It'd been many years, but the day remained seared in her soul, so much so that many things that hadn't made sense when she was a child became clearer as she aged and understood more about the true nature of the galaxy.

Aiyn closed her eyes and let the memory take her.

*Her younger self's eyes fluttered open as she yawned. The seconds after that were confused. She was at the spaceport, and it took her a moment to remember how she'd gotten there.*

*Her father had picked her up and rushed her to an air speeder. He'd told her to go back to sleep, so she'd let her exhaustion retake her.*

*He'd seemed so frightened in recent days, and none of her friends came over to play anymore. Her father had forbade her to do anything but play in her room, except when he took her to the sprawling spaceport where he worked fixing ships. Even there, he made her wait in an office and play with a doll. He wouldn't even let her have an AllBand.*

*She wasn't sure what bad thing she'd done, or how she'd made her father angry. That was the only explanation for why he was forcing her to stay in her room and wouldn't let her use an AllBand.*

*Now they were at the spaceport again, but he'd never before grabbed her at night and taken her there. She stared at the silver AllBand around her father's wrist longingly.*

*All those thoughts swirled through her head as the door to the already-grounded speeder slid open. Aiyn's father grabbed her hand and pulled her out of the vehicle.*

*A crush of people rushed toward the massive open hangar in front of her. Only a handful of shuttles remained inside. The squat, bulky short-range craft were disappointing compared to some of the sleek ships her father had shown her in happier times.*

*Aiyn gasped as something far more impressive caught her eye. Dozens, maybe hundreds, of huge transports hung in the sky, like a cluster of oblong metal clouds. She'd never seen so many ships above the city at once.*

*Huge lines of people stood in the gleaming hangar, rushing into the open shuttles one by one as the doors opened. Some wore grim expressions, others sobbed.*

*Several loud, distant booms sounded. Her father sucked in a breath and looked in that direction. She followed his gaze.*

*"I should have never stayed," he murmured. "Even if they needed help to get more ships ready, I should have never stayed. I didn't think they would get to the capital so fast. I thought they'd hold them farther to the south. They told us they would."*

*Dark smoke billowed up from the city, shrouding the gleaming crystal spires and dulling their light—at least the ones that weren't already collapsed. If it weren't for the red-orange glow over the city, the night might have swallowed it. Distant shiny dots zoomed back and forth, bright white light blasting from them toward the city below. A few green beams shot into the sky, turning the shiny dots into red flares for a moment.*

*Aiyn's eyes widened. "What's going on, Father?"*

*He frowned. "Don't worry about anything." He pointed at the transports. "We're leaving soon. We just need to get to a shuttle."*

*There was another loud boom, this time closer. Screams and shouts erupted from the crowd.*

*"They're coming!" a man yelled.*

*A massive energy bolt shot upward, bathing the entire hangar in a green glow, and struck one of the transports. The resulting massive explosion blew the ship into a cloud of debris, and three huge burning chunks fell to the ground. Her stomach tightened. She knew all too well what she was seeing. She also knew how many thousands of people could fit on a transport. Her father had told her.*

*"What's going on?" she cried.*

*"Damn it," her father muttered. "Six of them. There are only six of those monsters! How can thousands of our soldiers lose to six?"*

*"Six of who?"*

*He shook his head, his breathing ragged. "Evil monsters. Don't worry. We're escaping. They can't follow us into space. They travel a different way."*

*Monsters. Not mere enemies, but monsters.*

*Aiyn's heart pounded, and her shaking became uncontrollable.*

Protect us, Spirits. Protect us from the monsters.

*Several of the transports slowly pulled out of orbit.*

*"They're leaving," someone in the crowd screamed. "They're leaving us to die."*

*A herd charged the shuttles, people throwing the uniformed men monitoring entry to the side or punching and kicking them. Some of the crowd trampled others or shoved them out of the way. Panic gripped almost everyone.*

*Her father scooped Aiyn into his arms and rushed toward the closest shuttle. The sea of people around them jostled and bumped them, but no one knocked them over.*

*Tears blurred her vision, but she managed not to wail in her father's ear.*

*Another bolt passed overhead. A second ship exploded, turning night into day. Some of the shuttles in the hangar lifted off, the dull pulsing hum of their grav drives echoing in the hangar.*

*Their boarding doors remained open. A desperate man clung with one hand as one ship zoomed out of the hangar, falling with a scream to his death. In a similar situation, another passenger pulled a woman hanging from the door into the vehicle. The door slid closed, and the shuttle shot out of the hangar.*

*Aiyn stared, her blood pounding in her ears. The last few shuttles lifted off, clearly not at full capacity. People screamed and cursed. Some fell to their knees, sobbing and burying their faces in their hands.*

We're all going to die here. Monsters are going to kill us.

*Something thudded close behind her. A moment later, a green beam cut through the remaining hovering shuttles. The bisected vehicles rained to the ground, sending the people below scrambling. They weren't fast enough. Debris crushed dozens of people, their screams forming a haunting chorus.*

*The girl slowly turned her head. An armored figure stood in the distance, the glow of the burning city highlighting it. Silver-green metal covered its entire body and a featureless helmet covered its head, or maybe it* was *its head. Claws tipped its hands, and sharp blades extended from both arms. She wasn't sure if she was looking at armor or the skin of the monster.*

*The figure roared. The sound twisted her stomach, and Aiyn's lip quivered.*

*Her father spun around and hissed, then sprinted from the hangar toward a door in the distance. Something dark flew through the sky, arcing toward the other monster. The new arrival landed near the first monster with a thump and crouched as if it'd leapt a huge distance.*

*Aiyn trembled in her father's arms as he continued running, his labored breathing loud in her ear. It helped distract her from the horror of two of the monsters being so close.*

*Green sparks flowed around the blades of both monsters, a loud hum building as the glare of the sparks intensified. Energy flowed from each monster toward a central point between them. A small dot grew into a blinding ball of energy.*

*Her father broke into a mad rush toward the doorway.*

*The energy ball shot away from the monsters and smashed into the hangar roof. A massive explosion ripped through the entire structure, the shockwave knocking Aiyn and her father to the ground. She screamed as her arm snapped.*

*The remnants of the hangar crashed to the ground. Smoke and dust billowed out, coating the few survivors. Shattered crystal shards of the building lay everywhere, some having impaled victims.*

*Her father hopped up and wiped away some of the green blood gushing from the side of his head, then slung his daughter over his shoulder and started running again. Her broken arm dangled and each bump produced a new jolt of pain, but the carnage before her eyes dulled her anguish. Half the building had collapsed, burying thousands of people. Even the few people she could see laying on the ground were covered in soot and debris. All were motionless.*

*Both monsters roared and raised their arms to feed a new destructive blast.*

*Her father rushed through the shattered doorway and veered into a hallway on his right. The entire area shook again, flame and heat knocking him to his knees. Aiyn let out another scream as her arm shook. Tears poured down her face.*

*"We're almost there. Just hold on," her father whispered into her ear. "I should have brought you here to begin with. Or we should have left, but I wanted to do my part. But I have a plan to escape. It's why I've faked the maintenance records these last few days. You'll have a way out. I promise you that, Aiyn. No matter what else happens, you'll have a way out. It's very small. You'll escape, especially with so many transports left to draw their attention."*

*It was hard enough to understand what he was saying even without the pain overwhelming her concentration. She could only respond with sobs. They continued down twisting hallway after twisting hallway. Additional explosions rocked the building. Smoke choked the air.*

*The moments stretched to eternity, the pain killing even her ability to cry before her father arrived at a new smaller hangar. A single bright-silver triangular ship was parked there, shorter and thinner than any of the shuttles.*

*Burning debris and chunks of metal and crystal littered the hangar. Her father ran up to the ship and tapped his AllBand. The side of the ship slid open, revealing a single reclined seat.*

*"I'm sorry. This is going to hurt." Her father shoved her into the seat, jarring her arm.*

*She screamed.*

*His face a grim mask, her father ran his finger down a panel on the side of her seat. A dark harness extended from the four corners of the seat and secured her.*

*He leaned in to kiss her forehead. "I love you, Aiyn, and I'm sorry, but when your mother died, I promised her that I'd never let anything happen to you, no matter what the cost."*

*She stared at him, her vision clouded by her tears and mind addled by the pain.*

*Her father stepped back, and the side of the ship slid closed. A glowing holographic display lit up the cockpit.*

*"Initiating automated launch protocol," a soft female voice announced.*

*"Father," Aiyn cried before the pain and darkness overwhelmed her.*

---

*With a groan, Aiyn's eyes fluttered open. She gasped. A helmeted alien with four legs and two arms stood over her, his dark carapace gleaming almost like metal. Her heart rate kicked up, and a few seconds passed before she realized it wasn't a monster from the spaceport but an Alliance race, a Techain.*

*She'd never seen one of their kind in person before. The universal Alliance symbol for doctor decorated a white band around one of his arms.*

*The Techain tilted his head, the thick gasses inside his breather helmet hiding most of his face except for the dull red of his many eyes. He spoke, and the clicks and buzzes of his native language were translated by his helmet with a slight delay.*

*"You are safe now, child. You are on an Alliance cruiser far away from the Vax."*

*"Vax?" Aiyn croaked.*

*"The race that attacked your planet." The alien tilted his head back and forth several times, a few untranslated buzzes and clicks accompanying the motion. "We detected an automated distress signal from your ship when we arrived in-system, along with a signal requesting initiation of remote control. We were surprised to find a child inside. Your vessel was intended for diplomatic couriers."*

*Aiyn didn't understand everything the insectoid doctor had said, but she understood that her father had saved her.*

*"My father works at the spaceport. He fixes ships." Aiyn sat up and rotated her arm. The pain was gone. "Like you fixed my arm. Thank you."*

*"It is my duty."*

*Aiyn looked around. Several medical beds and tanks lined the narrow room. The tanks were empty, but her people filled the beds, most unconscious. Silver nanofoam covered their wounds. Small spherical drones buzzed around the room, stopping over patients for a few seconds before continuing.*

*"My father is dead, isn't he?" she whispered.*

*The Techain inclined his head. "I will attempt to find you a priestess of your religion if you require assistance with grieving. I am sorry for your loss."*

*Aiyn only could muster a shallow nod, her body numb.*

---

The adult Aiyn opened her eyes and wiped away a few tears. She fed the memory as much and often as she could.

*Never forgive. Never forget.*

She wanted to remember every sound, every sight, every smell. She needed to remember.

She laid her head on the bed and stared at her ceiling. "No more victims. No more orphans. I'll kill you, you Vax bastard, even if I have to strangle you myself."

## CHAPTER TWO

James stepped out of his F-350. The night air nipped at him, not freezing, but cold enough for Los Angeles. He was wearing a jacket, and not even to carry extra weapons and ammo. December was finally making itself known.

*Could be worse. Could be in Canada. Too much damned snow.*

There were many things to love and hate about LA, but one strong point in the city's favor was freedom from dreaded snow. The sky dandruff did nothing but make life complicated, whether it was driving or walking—let alone barbecuing. Every time a Christmas song extolled the virtues of snow and winter wonderlands, James understood a little bit better why the Grinch might be right.

*Someday Shay's gonna make me go to Antarctica. Shit.*

Thomas barked from the back seat, pulling James out of his weather-related reflection. The dog barked a few more times, his tail thumping against the leather. James grunted and nodded to the ground. The dog jumped out of the truck and padded over to his master's side.

James grabbed a leash from the seat and connected it to the dog's collar. Thomas obeyed his commands without question and didn't need the leash, but James understood how a large tattooed man with a decent-sized dog could make normal people nervous. Some old woman had called the police on him last time he went to the pet store to buy dog food, so he'd switched stores.

*Hope nothing happens this time.*

Buying his dog food online didn't appeal to him. He wanted to make sure his dog got a chance to look at the bag and sniff it a little. Thomas might not be picky, but he should at least have some input about what was going into his body.

James and Thomas walked to the front of the pet store. The glass doors slid open, and they entered the brightly lit building. Dozens of shelf-filled aisles lay in carefully arranged rows from the front to the back of the store. A small room with glass walls was to his right, a large PET GROOMING CENTER sign hanging on the door, although no groomers or pets were inside.

Thomas didn't need the service anytime soon. James had that taken care of a few days after finally finding the dog.

"Welcome, sir!" a cheerful redhead in a blue uniform called from the front register. "Maggie," according to her nametag. "Do you need help finding anything?"

He shook his head. "Nah, we're good. Come on, Thomas."

Maggie smiled at the dog. "Such a nice boy."

Thomas barked.

James led the dog down the aisles until he arrived at the dog section. He released the leash and squatted to inspect the various brands of dog food with a frown. His online research had pointed to different brands with different strengths. With Leeroy, he'd never worried that much, but with this dog, he worried about making sure he was doing his best to take care of him. Thomas didn't seem to be picky, but it wasn't like a dog could comment on nutrition.

"This one got good reviews." James leaned forward to peer at a large blue bag featuring a happy-looking Golden Retriever. "But I don't know if there's enough protein in there for you." He nodded to the bag. "Dogs need protein. Shit, humans need protein."

Thomas padded over to the bag and sniffed. He tilted his head and looked up at James, a question in his eyes.

"You'd probably eat cat food if I gave it to you. I'm trying to give you better choices here. Work with me." James grunted and continued his perusal of dog food for a few minutes before settling on the first bag, protein concerns aside.

He lifted the bag and stepped out of the aisle, leash in his other hand. After a moment of hesitation, he continued deeper into the store and away from the dog supplies. "Might as well check out some other shit while I'm here."

James approached a wall of terrariums, each containing a different variety of reptile or amphibian: bearded dragons, turtles, chameleons, geckos, and iguanas. The animals scampered in their glass enclosures, some fleeing, some watching him. A tranquil turtle sat staring through the glass at nothing in particular.

"Must be nice to not care about anything." James leaned forward to stare the turtle down. The animal didn't react. "So I've got you, Thomas. Should I get another new pet? Change-my-life kind of shit?"

Thomas barked once. James wasn't sure if that was agreement or objection.

James glanced at a different terrarium as a gecko skittered back and forth behind its glass. No one had ever said lizards were man's best friend.

With a shake of his head, he stepped away from the terrariums and turned the corner into a huge alcove filled with fish tanks. Colorful varieties of every type were represented, including glowing genetically engineered varieties and even an Oriceran species with oscillating patterns of light on the side.

James moved from tank to tank, watching the fish swim.

"How are these even a pet?" He grunted. "I mean, it's right there in the name: pet. You don't pet fish." He frowned. "They are glorified decorations. I don't need more decorations."

Thomas didn't bark any commentary.

"But maybe Shay would like some?" James rubbed the back of his neck. "Nah. That's bullshit. She likes you okay, but she's not big on pets. Yeah, no fish."

James led his dog away from the fish and down the avian aisle where bright birds stood on perches in glass display cases—mostly conures, parakeets, and cockatiels, nothing large. A small Oriceran species with four wings and blue eyes watched him, rigid as a statue. In contrast, the Earth birds tilted their heads, watching James with what he perceived as curiosity.

"Birds are pretty smart, and more than decorations." James shook his head. "Huh. Not decorations, but so damned small." He could always go to a specialty store and buy a large parrot. "It'd be weird if my bird suddenly started cussing at me, and Shay would teach it to fuck with me, too. Probably have it talking trash about Jessie Rae's."

James shook his head and looked down at Thomas. "No other pets. I think God planned for me to be a dog man."

Thomas barked.

"Yeah, thought you'd agree. Maybe I can get you a brother someday."

The dog tilted his head and didn't bark.

James grunted. "What, jealous already?"

Loud shouts came from the front of the door.

He frowned. "Wonder what that's about? Let's pay for your food and get the hell out of here. Can't believe people are starting shit at the pet store. Probably another old woman frowning at someone for having tattoos."

James led Thomas toward the front. Two lanky men in long coats stood at the front register, gesticulating wildly. Two bags of dried cat food were on the counter.

"What the fuck?" one of the men shouted, gesturing to the bags. "It clearly says twenty percent off if you buy two bags, so why the hell is it full price?"

James stared at the bag. "Huh. Didn't even think about a cat," he murmured. "Yeah, no way. Shay's always bitching about Peyton's cat."

Maggie offered a placating smile to the man, her hands in front of her. "I'm sorry, sir, but if you review the sign, you'll see that promotion applies only to specific brands. If you want to go back and grab bags from the participating brands, I'll be happy to give you a discount."

The man slapped his palm on the counter. Maggie winced and shrank back.

A few lingering customers eyed the exchange with concern on their faces, but no one stepped forward to help her.

"My cat doesn't like those other brands," the man growled. "She likes *this* fucking brand. A pet store employee is telling me to feed my beloved cat shit food she doesn't like?"

Maggie swallowed. "Sir, I'm afraid I'm going to have to ask you to leave. Your behavior is passing into verbal abuse."

The two men exchanged looks and laughed.

The first man sneered at her. "What did you say, bitch?"

With the exception of James, the other customers ducked into the aisles. One kneeling man pulled out a phone and whispered into it. A staff door at the side opened, and an older man in glasses poked his head out before ducking back inside and closing the door.

*Fucking coward. It's your employee.*

James let out a low growl. All he wanted to do was pay for his dog's food. That should have been a straightforward task, but Cat Fancier and his friend had fucked his night up.

*Should I wait for the police? Probably five to ten minutes for a cop to get here. By then it'll be too late.*

The thug leaned forward, a feral grin on his face. "I'm not fucking leaving, bitch. I'm offended by how you've disrespected my cat, and now you're gonna pay."

James grunted and released Thomas' leash. He walked toward the register. It was time to end this bullshit and get back home.

The first man whipped out a pistol and pointed it at the employee. Her hands shot into the air.

The second man pulled out a gun and spun, waving it around. "No one fucking move."

Several people screamed and dropped to the floor, their hands over their heads. James jaw's tightened.

*Big fucking mistake, asshole. I just wanted to buy some dog food.*

"Fine, if you won't give us a twenty percent discount," the first thug explained, "we'll take a hundred percent discount, bitch."

James snorted and advanced.

Both men spun to face him, angry confusion on their faces. They looked him up and down, but no recognition dawned.

"What's so fucking funny, meathead?" the first thug shouted. "You trying to be a hero?"

James nodded toward the register. "Who the fuck robs a pet store? She's not going to have shit for actual cash in there, and you guys don't look like you have the equipment for electronic transfers, so you're going to steal a bunch of cat food? You're risking going to prison over a twenty percent discount, dumb shit."

The thug pointed his gun directly at James' head. "Keep talking and you die, motherfucker. Do you know who I am? Do you know how many people I've killed?" The thug narrowed his eyes.

Thomas barked loudly at the thug. He crept forward, poised to lunge at the man threatening his master.

The thug glared at the dog. "You stupid-ass furry piece of shit. I fucking hate dogs anyway." He pointed his gun at Thomas. "Time to see if all dogs go to heaven."

James sprang forward. He grabbed the man's arm and yanked it up so hard it popped out of its socket.

The man yowled in pain, and his yowls turned to screams as James squeezed slowly. The muscles and tendons compressed under his grip. He released the man, and the thug's gun fell.

"The real question you should be asking, motherfucker," James offered, the grinding machinery quality of his voice even more pronounced than usual, "is who *I* am and how many people *I* have fucking killed?"

The other thug backed up, his eyes wide and his hands shaking, the gun along with them. "W-who the fuck are you, man?"

"I'm James Brownstone, and I just wanted to buy some fucking dog food." He grabbed the first thug again and tossed him at his friend.

The groaning man collided with a thud, and both men fell to the ground. The second thug's gun clattered to the tile and came to rest a yard away from his hand.

James stalked forward, his eyes narrowed. "And you might have heard how I don't like it when people hurt my dog."

The first thug lay on his side, groaning in pain. "Fucker. My hand. My arm."

"Because you didn't actually hurt my dog you don't die,

asshole. But you need to learn proper motherfucking respect for man's best friend."

The thug's partner shook his head and sat up. He blinked a few times before scrambling for the gun, but James surged forward and introduced his boot to the man's chest. The thug flew back and smashed through the window, the shattered glass raining down around him.

Thomas barked and wagged his tail.

*We both like a good ass-kicking, huh?*

James rounded on the first man, knelt, and slammed a fist into the thug's face. The thug's head snapped back, smacking against the hard tile with an audible thud, and he slumped, unconscious.

Maggie gaped at James, wide-eyed.

After taking a deep breath, he headed to the counter and set down the dog food bag. "You okay?"

She nodded quickly. "Y-yes, sir."

James grunted. "Add a few thousand for the window. If it costs more than that to fix it, let me know. Just call the Brownstone Agency and tell my administrative assistant Charlyce."

"Okay, sir." Maggie blinked a few times. "But I'm going to have to ask my manager how to enter that into the register."

# CHAPTER THREE

James stepped out of the garage into the hallway. Thomas rushed into the living room to claim his preferred spot on the floor while his owner pressed his phone to his ear.

"Did you really need to throw them through a window, James?" asked Sergeant Mack on the other end, his voice exasperated.

James grunted. "I'll pay for all the damages."

"Okay, the staff seem grateful for your intervention and your willingness to pay for everything, but you can't go busting up normal places even if they threaten your dog or pull guns on you. You could have just disabled them. You have to show restraint."

"I *did* show restraint. I didn't kill them. Didn't even come close." James frowned.

He hadn't even broken the first guy's arm. That had been saintly restraint. Sure, Father McCartney would probably still caution him about wrath during confession, but his soul was a work in progress.

Sergeant Mack chuckled. "There *is* that. Anyway, I'll handle the paperwork on the police end, but just keep what I said in mind. Even with your reputation, there's only so much we can keep out of the press."

"I'll keep it in mind," James replied. "Doesn't mean I won't beat down any fucker dumb enough to threaten my dog and some innocent cashier. People need to learn their fucking lessons. I would have figured destroying the Harriken made that clear on the dog part."

Sergeant Mack sighed. "I'm sure if those idiots had known who they were messing with they wouldn't have done anything. Okay, got to go. I'll see you in a couple of weeks for our PFW planning meeting."

"See you then." James ended the call and shook his head.

Maybe his friend had a point. It wasn't the pet shop's fault some fucker had threatened his dog. He shouldn't have used their window as a weapon.

James nodded to himself. Next time, he wouldn't kick someone who threatened his dog through a window, he'd break his arms and legs. That shouldn't cause much trouble, even if he were at a florist.

*Why the fuck would I be buying flowers? Shay doesn't even like that shit.*

He decided it didn't matter. At least now he had a plan in the unlikely event he was in a flower shop with Thomas, and someone was willing to threaten his dog there.

"No, no, no," Shay shouted from inside.

James rushed into the living room. Shay's face was contorted into a mask of rage. She paced the living room, her phone in her hand.

She let out a strangled growl. "I thought we were *way* past this point, Peyton."

James frowned and crossed his arms. He liked Shay's hacker well enough, but if he were fucking with his woman, he deserved whatever beatdown she delivered.

"Because it's obviously not that simple," Shay shouted into her phone. "And I don't *care* if you're the God of all Hacking. If that place starts burning, the fucking cops and firefighters are going to show up." She frowned and tilted her head. "No, that's not a damned excuse. Do not burn down my warehouse because that damned cat distracted you by being *fucking cute*." She groaned. "Just don't let it happen again, Pizza King." She ended the call and dropped her phone into her pocket.

"Need any help?" James asked.

Shay took a deep breath and scrubbed a hand over her face. "That guy is a fucking genius half the time, but then shit like this happens." She shook her head and waved a hand. "It's fine. Sometimes I need to remind him who's boss. Find the dog food?"

James nodded. "Yeah, it was pretty simple."

He shrugged. No reason to make his night more complicated by mentioning he had kicked a man through a window.

A smile spread over Shay's face, erasing the anger. "And on a happier note, just a few weeks until Alison's home. Excited?"

James took a seat on the couch and eyed Thomas. The dog was already sleeping.

"Yeah, glad to have her back. I know that school's good

for her, but I also feel like she's changing there, and I don't always know what's going through her head now."

Shay laughed and sat beside him. She patted his shoulder. "That's called growing up, James. Your little girl's becoming a woman and all that, and more importantly, your little Drow princess is coming into her power, too. That was why you sent her there."

James grunted. "I know." He frowned. "Wonder if we should be doing something special for Christmas break? Going somewhere. I fucking hate snow, but maybe she wants a white Christmas or shit like that."

"Doubt it. She grew up here." Shay worked her mouth a little and nodded. "Though it might be a good time for us to go somewhere. I was wondering if some new crazy-ass monster would show up to threaten you, but since you blew up that amusement park and defeated the last of the Council, things have been quiet."

"I didn't blow up the amusement park. I destroyed one ride." James shrugged. "There were those level fours a few weeks back, but yeah, guess you're right. Trey, Maria, and the guys have been able to handle everything else."

Shay nodded. "I was thinking, you know, you and me and Alison could actually take a true winter vacation. I've only done one raid since that last one with Lily. It's not like either of us has to work right away to pay rent. Yeah, I'll admit I like a rush now and again, but you know, if it helps you…"

James frowned. "Helps me what?"

"Step back a little." She shrugged. "You said it yourself—your agency's dealing with trouble, both here and in Vegas. The shit they handled with the Council gave them the kind of experience that a lot of AET and PDA don't have. You're expanding the agency and looking into new recruits." She pointed at James. "You don't have to personally push back the tsunami of assholes that always threatens to swallow this city."

James furrowed his brow. "What are you saying? You want me to stop being a bounty hunter? Are you going to stop being a tomb raider?"

"Not saying that, but I'm considering cutting back." Shay blew out a breath. "Look, the thing is, I became a tomb raider for money, but also because I love history. It was a natural fit. I did so many raids before because I was trying to disappear and needed the money. Now I'm not, and I don't." She smiled at him. "I have a reason to stay around. Even thought about trying to do more at the university. Definitely still doing raids, if only to scratch that itch, but if *I* can start thinking about cutting back, maybe you should, too."

"What would I do with my time?" James nodded to the curled up and comatose Thomas. "He doesn't want to play with me that much."

Shay gestured to the tv. "Watch barbeque shows, dream about your truck, or shit like that. Why not go through with the whole barbeque restaurant plan? Your team has placed well at competitions. You would come in with a reputation."

James leaned back on the couch, thinking the whole thing over. A year ago, he'd dismissed the idea as something for the far future, but now something about the idea appealed, including a regular life: more time with Shay and fewer concerns about if some asshole would go after his daughter or his woman in revenge for him beating them down.

He grunted and shook his head. "Already pressing my luck as it is."

"Pressing your luck? What do you mean?" Shay frowned.

"I've barely been able to go a month without some fucking asshole messing with me or getting dragged into some messed-up shit." James snorted. "If I opened a barbeque place, some dragon would show up three weeks into it and burn it down. I've been thinking about He Who Hunts, and how it's been too long. It's like, if I don't constantly beat assholes down, they forget not to fuck with me. Just like those two fuckers in the pet store."

Shay narrowed her eyes. "What two fuckers in the pet store?"

"Two guys decided they were going to rob the pet store. One of them threatened to shoot Thomas."

"And what did you do?"

James shrugged. "Crushed one's hand and knocked his ass out. Kicked the other through a window."

Shay rolled her eyes. "Oh, you're worried about that? You didn't kill those guys. For you, that's restraint."

"Just saying, they fucked with me." James grunted. "Not saying I'm worried about that shit, just that maybe a restaurant wouldn't be the best idea."

"They didn't happen to recognize you?" Shay sighed and let her head fall against the back of the couch. "Now you've gotten into my head. Thanks. I needed that."

"Gotten into your head? What are you talking about?"

Shay turned her head to look at him. "Brownstone-

Carson luck. Since I killed Snegurka and backed off a bit on the alien shit, there are very few people actively trying to fuck with me. Then again, I try to keep a low profile in my day job. I don't think you and 'low profile' belong in the same county."

James shrugged. "Got to be me. I don't think I'm gonna start becoming quieter when I beat fuckers down."

She laughed. "Yeah." She jerked upright and snapped, "I've got it. An idea."

James stared at her. "Huh?"

"Even if we, or even you, don't really have bad luck, we're both gonna obsess over it because of all the shit we've had to deal with." Shay shook a finger. "But we can reset our luck, or at least our perception of it."

"I have no fucking idea what you're talking about, and I'm not obsessing over shit. I just don't think it makes sense to open a barbeque restaurant."

Shay grinned. "Instead of waiting for a major ass-kicking to come our way, let's go find one."

James grunted, now more confused than ever. "When I did the pay-per-view thing with Tyler you got pissed, and now you want me to go looking for trouble?"

She rolled her eyes. "That's not what I'm talking about. I'm saying we go find a job, something we can both do—maybe a joint tomb raid and bounty hunt. His-and-hers ass-kicking. Like when I met you." She smirked. "It'll be sweet. You can kill a bunch of twisted fucks, and I can find some cool ancient artifact lost to history. I bet if we called up Smite-Williams he'd have something. Then we can get it out of both our systems and enjoy Christmas break with Alison without having that nagging worry in the back of our mind about shit hanging over us."

"I'm not worried." James rubbed the back of his neck. "But I'll think about it."

Shay laughed. "Don't think too long or that dragon will show up and burn your house down."

---

Trey patted his stomach and leaned back in his chair at Zoe's dining room table. He set his fork down on his plate, which was still half-covered with his third serving of cheese tortellini. "That was some damned fine pasta. It's delicious, but I just can't eat anymore without exploding, and then you'd have Trey guts all over your dining room. It'd just be hard to clean up. Can't do that to you."

Zoe chuckled and folded her hands in front of her. "I lived in Italy for a few decades. I tried to take advantage of my time there to learn new skills."

He laughed. "Of course you did. Works for me. You learned what you needed during all those years, and that's what makes you such an interesting woman."

She gave him a flirtatious smile. "You're still leaving soon for Las Vegas?"

Trey nodded. "Yeah. For now, still doing the same thing we've always done. We all take our turns, and especially since we lost Shorty, they need me to be there more. Maria's stepping into the other leadership role, but she's focused a lot on tactical training."

Her smile faded. "So you're going to Vegas, but James won't be going, will he?"

“Big man don’t need to be there.” Trey shrugged. “We’ve got ass-kicking down to a science. He deserves some time off.”

Zoe held up a hand. “Wait here.” She stood, moved toward the door, and disappeared into her living room.

Trey eyed his pasta again, trying to work up the will to go in for another bite, but his gurgling stomach made its opinion clear. He sat in the dining room waiting for his girlfriend to return and drumming his fingers on the table.

*Is this one of those things where she comes back in naked?*

She re-emerged with a pair of black leather gloves.

*Is she gonna take off everything but the gloves?*

Zoe held them out. “I should have perhaps asked about your preferences before, but I think you’ll like the color, at least. A gift.”

They were almost as nice as a hot, naked witch. Almost.

“They look damned sweet to me. Yeah, been getting colder. Nice to have a new pair of gloves to keep my trigger finger warm.” Trey grinned and took the gloves.

A hint of color on the inside caught his attention. He set one on the table and pulled the other’s opening wider. Intricate blue glyphs were sewn inside the gloves.

Trey furrowed his brow and looked at Zoe. “This looks magical.”

“Training can do much, my little supernova,” the witch declared, batting her gray eyes. “But there are natural differences in power between people, especially in the world we live in. I know you well enough now to understand that you’ll continue to aspire to further greatness, if only because of the brightness of the fire of your employer.”

Trey stared at the gloves. "The big man is badass. Not gonna apologize for wanting to be more like him. What do these gloves have to do with that?"

"I'm a specialist in potions, to the point where I make better potions than many, many witches far more powerful than me." Zoe sat in her chair and crossed her legs, the slit in her dress providing a peek of her thigh. "So I can help you with potions, but my skill in things like enchanted gloves is low, so I traded some favors and had those made for you. They are not as powerful as whatever *he* might be using, but they will increase your ability both to inflict and take punishment. Be cautious. They aren't infinite in use, but they will recharge themselves if you simply leave them be."

Trey held up a glove. "You're saying these are genuine magical artifacts?"

Zoe nodded. "I should also note they'll only harden your skin against attacks, not your clothes. Please also keep in mind that they only work for you. The magic will not respond to anyone else."

"Sad for my poor suits." Trey grinned. "But why? This shit had to be expensive as hell, even if you were trading favors."

"I decided to devote myself to you, and I've found myself to be not disappointed in either your power or your attention to me as a woman." Zoe gave him a soft smile. "I have an investment in you now since I doubt I'll be able to find another man like you anytime soon, so it's important that I keep you alive as long as possible, my little supernova."

Trey shrugged, satisfied. He blinked as he realized something he'd missed before. "No wine tonight?"

"I wanted to have a clear memory of the gift. Every time you leave this city, I find myself worrying." Zoe inhaled slowly, half-closing her eyes. "This is the difficulty with my tastes. I'm attracted to fiery men, but your very nature will bring you into contact with danger."

"Hey, if I've got a fine witch backing me up, I'm gonna keep coming back home alive. You don't have to worry."

Zoe licked her lips. "So I tell myself. There's another reason I didn't need to drink tonight."

Trey slipped the gloves into his pocket. "And what's that, Zoe?"

"Because you're going to give me a little power," Zoe murmured. She ran a hand over her thigh. "Perhaps a little fun on the table?"

"Now, don't get me wrong. I don't plan on leaving this house without making so much steam with you that people will think this place is a greenhouse, but..." Trey turned and frowned at a tall blue plant covered in wide leaves with prominent purple veins in the corner of the room.

It twitched, its leaves curling and uncurling.

"What?" Zoe asked.

Trey nodded toward the plant. "Can't do it nowhere those freaky Oriceran plants might be watching."

"Would it help if I told you they aren't intelligent?"

He laughed. "Nope. Gonna have to settle for me rocking your world in the bedroom."

Zoe stood and licked her lips. "A sacrifice I'm willing to make."

## CHAPTER FOUR

"What the fuck is up with that look on your face, Trey?" Daryl asked as he pulled the Expedition to the curb up the street from a body shop, their target for that evening. "You've been looking like that from the moment we drove into fucking Vegas. You have some system you can use to beat all the casinos?"

"Nah, nothing like that." Trey shrugged. "And nothing wrong with my face. Not everyone can be a hater like you."

Lachlan laughed from the back seat. "You don't know what's going on, Daryl?"

The other bounty hunter snorted. "It's just fucking freaking me out. He's all grinning like he's high or some shit."

"Can you get high from giving a little somethin'-somethin' to a witch?" Kevin asked from beside Trey.

Trey snorted. "Fuck all y'all. I ain't gonna feel bad because my girlfriend is hot and magical. Fuck, probably rich, too, even if she lives in that tiny little house." He reached into the pockets of his black suit and pulled out the gloves. "She's all worried and shit, so she set me up."

Daryl glanced his way. "Meaning what? Special potions?"

"Yeah, I got some of that shit, too, but these are magic fucking gloves. Make me stronger and tougher."

Kevin eyed the gloves appreciatively. "You should change your nickname from Trey the Gigolo to Trey Brownstone."

Everyone laughed, including Trey.

He shook his head. "Nah, I ain't like the big man, but this is the kind of shit we're all gonna need to move into his league. Maria's helping train our asses, so we can think like SWAT and AET, and the big man's giving us deflectors and anti-magic bullets when we need them, but look at how he fights. It ain't always about shooting and shit. Sometimes you need to beat a motherfucker down, you know what I'm sayin'?"

"I ain't complaining that you're more badass now," Lachlan offered with a shrug. "I just didn't realize you impressed that witch so much. Damn, Trey, you're a fucking *machine* if she's giving you magic artifacts."

Trey slipped on the gloves. "I played around with them a little bit, but now I get the chance to test them out for real. Still not gonna purposely get shot, though." He slapped a gloved hand against the bulletproof vest underneath his jacket. "We need suits that are bulletproof without vests. This shit just don't look as good."

The others chuckled and shook their heads.

Trey grinned. "Just a reminder—DeBois, Calloway, and Adams ain't got magic, but they are still dangerous motherfuckers and level threes." He patted his shoulder holster. "We're gonna grab the boys using non-lethals to get the payday, but you do what you need to do to protect your asses. Shit, and the rest of your body."

Lachlan snorted. "You figure these fuckers will give up when we say who we are? It's like our ancient Chinese brother said, 'To subdue the enemy without fighting is the acme of skill.'"

Trey gave a little snort. "We ain't there yet. We're *almost* there, but keep in mind even the big man still has fuckers who screw with him. Sergeant Mack told me he had to put some piece of shit who threatened to shoot Thomas through a window the other day."

The bounty hunters all glowered.

Kevin growled. "What motherfucker is going to take down Doggy Brownstone? We should pay them a visit and show them how we feel about that."

Trey threw up a hand. "Weren't you listening? Big man handled it. We don't need to do shit. The point is that there's no badder motherfucker on this planet than James Brownstone. Maybe there is on Oriceran, but who gives a shit, because that ain't Earth. And even with him being the baddest motherfucker on Earth, dumb shits still come and try to step up to him. So, yeah, it'd be cool and shit if fuckers would buy a clue about fighting the Brownstone Agency, but there will always be someone who does." He opened his door. "Let's arm up and do our thing."

The men nodded their agreement and hurried out of the vehicle, with Lachlan grabbing stun rifles from the back and handing them to each man. Soon, the four bounty hunters strode down the street, all in dark suits, though without their sunglasses, given the time of night.

Trey had complained about that a few times, suggesting maybe James invest in augmented-reality glasses with fancy night vision for all of them. It was one of the few times Trey's boss hadn't seemed interested in spending extra cash on his men.

*You don't need that shit. Sounds like you just want to look cool.*

Trey chuckled at the memory. James might be a badass, but the man had no sense of style.

They closed on the body shop. The lights inside were still on, but the bounty hunters lacked line-of-sight on the front window.

Trey spotted a camera. A jammer wouldn't do shit if it were on a hardline, and part of Maria's growing influence on the agency was restricting the use of expensive gear like EMPs to situations that warranted them to cut down on unnecessary expenses.

He didn't mind. He wasn't planning on sneaking up on the bastards anyway.

"Kevin, Daryl," Trey began, "you cover the back. Lachlan and I are gonna knock on the front door and say hello to our friends."

The other two bounty hunters nodded and sprinted toward the back of the brick building.

Trey and Lachlan strutted toward the front. If they were going to intimidate the men into surrendering, confidence would be key. They passed the front windows. A single man stood behind the counter, looking up not at a security monitor but a TV showcasing a boxing match between two Kilomea.

Lachlan grimaced. "Shit. I forgot all about that fight. I was gonna bet on that. Championship bout."

Trey snorted and threw open the front door. He stepped inside, followed by Lachlan. The burly man in stained coveralls wore a nametag that said Hank, but Trey recognized him as Luke DeBois, one of their targets.

After a few more punches between the boxers, DeBois spotted the bounty hunters, his brow knitting. "What the fuck?"

Trey lifted his stun rifle. "Don't like this shit, DeBois?"

"Who the fuck are you?" The bounty's hand edged underneath the counter.

"I'm Trey, and this is my associate Lachlan. We represent the Brownstone Agency. You've been a bad boy, Mr. DeBois. We'd like it if you surrendered without trouble." Trey grinned. "But for such a badass, you sure let us get the drop on you."

DeBois narrowed his eyes. His hand now rested underneath the counter and out of sight. "You have no idea who you're fucking with."

Trey shook his head. "Nah, that's just the thing. We do, Mr. Level Three."

The criminal's arm shot up, a pistol in hand.

Trey and Lachlan fired, the blue stun bolts blasting from the rifles. DeBois jerked to the side, the shots striking the wall behind him, and opened fire, the loud report of his pistol echoing in the front room. Two bullets struck Trey.

He winced at the pain and stumbled back, yanking his rifle to the side to lead his target and fired again. This time the stun bolt landed square in the criminal's chest. DeBois collapsed with a groan.

Lachlan put another bolt into him before rushing over to kick the gun out of his hand. He shouldered his rifle with a quick fling of the strap and knelt to handcuff the bounty. "Shit, you okay, Trey?"

The other bounty hunter took a few deep breaths. His chest was sore, but the ache felt more like a solid punch to the chest rather than the rib-breaking sledgehammer he'd experienced before in that situation.

"I'm fine." Trey grinned. "I wouldn't risk getting shot with my gloves without my vest, but stacking the shit is working nicely." He nodded to DeBois. "Keep an eye on him. I'm gonna go find his friends."

Even if Daryl and Kevin hadn't heard the modest buzz of the stun rifle, they would have heard DeBois' gunshot and rushed in the back. Trey didn't need Maria there to tell him the importance of a pincer attack.

Trey kicked open the door to the garage and flattened himself against the wall to peek around the corner. Two dented cars sat inside, one on a jack stand. He rushed around the corner, his rifle still over his shoulder.

*This shit might be dangerous, but if I don't test these gloves now, never gonna know how good they are.*

Someone shouted from a back hallway leading to the garage, and a few gunshots rang out.

"Fuck," Trey muttered.

He sprinted toward the hallway. His boys didn't have magic gloves. He had passed the dented car on the ground when someone sprang up from the front and swung a tire iron at his head.

The tool connected with a resounding thud and pain shot through the side of Trey's head. He dropped with a grunt and hissed in pain. After a few seconds, he shook his head and touched the side. It was slick with blood, and his head hurt, but he was still able to think.

*That shit should have knocked my ass clean out. Gonna need a little potion if I don't want stitches, but I'm still in the fight. These gloves are working out nicely.*

Trey hopped to his feet and glared at the shaven-headed man who'd hit him—another of the level threes, Calloway.

The man frowned, his hands tightening on the tire iron. "You've got a thick skull, bounty hunter."

"Nah, that ain't it." Trey grinned despite the pain in the side of the head. "I just know how to please a woman in bed."

Calloway's face scrunched. "What the fuck are you talking about?"

Trey lifted his gloved hands and smiled. "Fuck those Kilomea. Lachlan should've bet on *my* ass."

Kevin ran into the room.

"You take the other guy down?" Trey called.

Kevin frowned and nodded. He pointed his rifle at Calloway. "Just this asshole left."

Trey shook his head. "I need to test this shit, Kevin, so I'm gonna offer Calloway a little deal."

The criminal gritted his teeth and looked at Kevin and Trey.

"You ain't escaping right now, bitch." Trey flexed his fingers. "I've got one of my boys in the front and one in the back, even beyond Kevin there."

The other bounty hunter nodded.

"I can fucking kill you," Calloway growled.

"Yeah, that's it. That's what I'm talking about." Trey slid the strap of his rifle off his shoulder and tossed the weapon behind him. "Maria's always talking about getting tactical experience in all situations. Staff Sergeant says the same shit, and of course, our ancient Chinese brother says, 'If in training soldiers' commands are habitually enforced, the army will be well-disciplined.' He was talking more about formations and shit, but I think it applies to direct fighting experience, too."

The bounty stared at Trey. "What the fuck are you talking about? Who the fuck is Maria? What do the… What the fuck in general?"

Trey shook his head and clucked his tongue. "You should work on getting an education and a few ex-AET to help you. I'll lay it out for you, Calloway. I need to test something, and you are as good as anyone to help me." He patted the side of his head and hissed at the pain. "And you already proved you like to get up close and personal. I'm gonna take you on, you with your tire iron and just me with nothing but these gloves. If you beat me down, you can leave."

"Woah, Trey, what the fuck you talking about?" Kevin shouted.

"It's all right. Even if this fucker gets away tonight, we can track his ass down later. He ain't getting away." Trey grinned at the bounty. "So, how about it, Calloway? You got nothing to lose. Yo, Kevin, put down your rifle."

"Seriously, Trey?" Kevin shook his head. "This is dumb."

"Want to give him a chance to get away if he wins." Trey shrugged.

"I can see that he beat your ass already from over here. You got brain damage."

Trey flipped Kevin off. "I'll show you some brain damage, motherfucker." He turned back toward Calloway. "You ready, bitch?"

The criminal snorted. "You're fucking lucky you ain't dead already. I don't give a shit about your friends, I'm gonna wipe that fucking cocky-ass smile off your face, bounty hunter."

He charged and swung the tire iron. Trey jumped back, the tool missing by inches.

*Shit. To test this thing, gonna have to get hit on purpose. Glad I got an extra couple of potions from Zoe because this shit's gonna hurt.*

Calloway growled and rushed forward, launching another attack. Trey threw up his left arm to block. The tire iron connected, and he grunted as pain radiated from his arm.

The bounty hunter stumbled back and shook out his left arm. It had a dull throbbing ache, but his full range of motion had been preserved.

"That shit would have normally broken my arm, I think," Trey announced.

"What the fuck is going on?" Lachlan called from behind him.

"You supposed to be watching DeBois," Trey shouted. He kept his attention on the criminal in front of him. "Don't worry about me. Just testing my little present from my woman."

"You think because you went and bought yourself a

truck you're motherfucking James Brownstone? You ain't no Brownstone, bitch." Lachlan snorted.

Calloway waved his tire iron. "What the fuck? Is this how you do all your bounties? Fuck you all. I ain't no punk-ass bitch. You have any idea how many people I've killed?"

He growled and charged Trey. He took another huge swing and connected with Trey's left arm again. The bounty hunter stumbled, and Calloway smashed the arm again with a two-handed overhead swing. Pain exploded through Trey's left arm, and it jerked, now swinging freely.

Trey sprang up and slammed a fist squarely into the bounty's chest. The blow landed with a loud crunch, and Calloway wheezed. He sailed backward and slammed into the wall, his eyes rolling up in the back of his head before closing as he slid down it.

*Shit. Not the distance I've seen the big man get, but not bad at all.*

His breathing ragged, Trey reached into his pocket with his non-broken arm to pull out a healing potion. He pulled out the stopper with his teeth, spat it out, and downed the potion in one gulp.

Kevin hurried over to Calloway and knelt. He put his fingers to the man's throat to take his pulse.

"Shit," Trey muttered as the pain began to fade. "Didn't mean to kill the motherfucker."

"Did you mean to sit there and take that beating? I know you can fight better than that." Kevin shook his head. "That shit is crazy. You trust your girlfriend that much?"

Trey blinked a few times and rotated his now-healed left arm. "Guess I do."

Kevin rolled Calloway over and handcuffed him. "He's still alive. Next time don't take the beating first, Brownstone Junior."

Trey raised the gloves and grinned. "Yeah, I think I'll leave the punching through windows shit to the big man and stick to guns." He laughed. "Shit might help, but damned if it ain't still hurt like a motherfucker. Still..." He kissed his fingers and raised his hands. "Thanks, Zoe. This is sweet."

# CHAPTER FIVE

James skimmed through the messages on his phone as he leaned back in his recliner, Thomas slumbering beneath the raised footrest. Most messages concerned his barbeque team, but a few were from Trey, Maria, or Royce about agency matters. His people understood he was supposed to be on a vacation of sorts, and they were trying their best not to bother him with petty details.

It was easy to run a successful bounty hunting agency when everyone who worked for him was so damned good at what they did. Royce and Maria were currently putting a new group of trainees through the wringer—some of the security guards who'd stood their ground against He Who Hunts' forces at the amusement park. A man willing to face a monster without special training already had what it took to be polished into a badass bounty hunter.

He stopped and read a text from Trey. Zoe was giving him magical artifacts now. James wasn't sure if that was dangerous. Then again, the witch had suggested James was the dangerous one.

*Not like she's wrong.*

His gaze drifted to his chest. His shirt covered the amulet and a spacer separated it from his skin, but when James did wear it, Whispy Doom was bolder. He was becoming more insistent about his mysterious primary directive. The damned amulet would never spell out what that was, other than insisting James keep attacking people and adapting to their attacks.

*Does he just want me to be the strongest motherfucker on the planet? What the fuck happens when I achieve the primary directive? Does he leave?*

James grunted. He'd gone from hating the amulet and never wanting to use it to depending on it as a valuable weapon. As tough as he was, he wouldn't be able to take on a lot of higher-level bounties without Whispy Doom. That might not be a problem if he retired, but the more he thought about the idea, the less it appealed to him.

*A barbeque place might be nice, but I don't think I was put on this Earth to cook delicious fucking meat. Plenty of pitmasters out there who can handle that, but not a lot of guys like me.*

He rubbed the amulet through his shirt. He might not know the answers to all the questions concerning his past, but he knew he was an alien—and an especially powerful one with Whispy Doom's help.

*Maybe I've been wrong. The amulet gets off on me kicking ass, but he's not trying to get me to kill everyone in sight. If I'm supposed to get stronger, there might be a reason. Maybe it's about becoming the strongest person to protect Earth or some shit?*

James shook his head. He could think about the possibilities all day, but without more information from the damned amulet, it didn't matter how many guesses he came up with. For all he knew, he was on some intergalactic reality show where aliens tested what would happen if they dropped a kid somewhere with traumatic memories and a bloodthirsty amulet.

"With my luck, that's probably the truth." He snorted and pulled up his contacts list. Time to focus on something more positive. He dialed Alison.

"Hey, Dad," she answered cheerfully. "Mom told me you kicked a guy through a window?"

"He threatened Thomas."

"Oh," she replied, her voice cold. "He should be happy he's not dead."

"Exactly." James grunted. "But that's not what I wanted to talk about. Just wanted to make sure you were coming home for Christmas Break. If you want to go to one of your friends or some island or something, I'd understand."

"Some island?"

James grunted. "Yeah, you know, like the Caribbean."

"I want to see you and Mom," Alison insisted. "I don't see either of you enough. And I want to play with Thomas. If *you* want to go to the Caribbean, though, that's fine with me. It might be fun."

"I don't really know." He rubbed the back of his neck. "I've been talking to Shay about doing something special, but we're still figuring out what might work."

Alison laughed. "For a man who likes things to be simple, you sure manage to complicate them, Dad."

"Just saying." James frowned. "If you want to bring

someone, you can. If it's a boy, he has to sleep on the couch where Thomas can watch him."

"A boy?" Alison sighed. "Dad, it'll be a long time before I'll risk bringing any boy home to meet you."

"Why? Anyone you're interested in has to go through your parents eventually."

"Listen to yourself," Alison replied. "'Go through?' It's not a bounty or a war. The point is, asking a boy to visit you in LA at your house isn't just brave, it's suicidal. I think I need to be a hundred percent sure a boy's *the one* before I ask someone to risk facing James Brownstone. It's just not fair otherwise."

James snorted. "If they can't handle me, they don't deserve you." He looked over his shoulder to make sure Shay wasn't around.

"Maybe." A few seconds of silence passed. "But if we're talking about the future, I'm a teen, and you're the adult."

"Meaning what?"

"Meaning it might be nice for Shay to really become my mom," Alison murmured.

James frowned. "Oh, you want her to adopt you, too?"

Alison let out a long sigh. "Um, not exactly. Look, Dad, I have to go. I definitely want to come home for break. I'll be taking the train, and no, I'm not bringing any boys home. Talk to you later, and love you."

He felt like the conversation had slipped out of control somehow, but he didn't understand why.

"Okay, I love you too, Alison."

James stared at the dial pad, a deep frown on his face. Alison was pissed. That was the only explanation for why she'd rush off the phone.

*Why would she get upset about asking what I did? She's the one who said she wanted Shay to be her mom.*

He slipped his phone into his pocket. What else could it mean?

*Shit.*

James grunted. If he married Shay, she would become Alison's stepmother. She actually would become her mom.

He sat there, frozen by the enormity of it all. He couldn't deny he felt something strong for Shay and never wanted her to leave his life, but he wasn't human. As much as he feared the void of her leaving him, a long-term future seemed like an impossibly arrogant dream.

Shay suggested his amulet had modified him to pass for human, which was why DNA tests in the past hadn't revealed anything strange, but exotic Oriceran races had already proven some of the limitations of human molecular biology technology. If they got married, other logical next steps might affect his true nature.

*Just because a lot of Oricerans and humans can have kids doesn't mean every freak from another planet can.*

James shook his head. Insofar as he understood what love was, he loved Shay, and he couldn't burden her with a permanent anchor. He wasn't human. He wasn't even Oriceran.

*I'm sorry, Alison. I can't go that far, for Shay's sake.*

---

From behind the bar, Tyler eyed a busty blonde waitress as she made her way, tray of drinks in hand, to a group of Russian Mafia enforcers sitting in the corner.

"Keep leering, and I'll tell Maria," Kathy murmured from beside him.

Tyler snorted. "I'm not leering, I'm evaluating. It's been a while since I last had waitresses. Trying to figure out the best balance between expense and profit. Staffing levels. That sort of thing."

Kathy chuckled and cleared a few empty glasses off the bar. "There *is* such a thing as being too cheap, you know. It's not like you're just scraping by. You don't have to micromanage expenses that much."

"Of course I'm not just scraping by." Tyler puffed up his chest. "Because of my smart Brownstone-related investments, this place and my operation have gone from small-time to big-time, but it's not enough." He rubbed his chin. "I need to figure out a way to take my business to the next level, but this business model has inherent limitations."

A loud crash sounded over the rock playing on the speakers. Another new waitress was waving her hands in front of a table of police officers.

"I'm sorry. I'm sorry," the woman offered. "I'll get that cleaned up right away."

Tyler scrubbed a hand over his face. "That's the third time today."

"It's because you're hiring them for how they look." Kathy snorted. "Hire them for competence and experience, and you'll lose fewer glasses and less booze."

Tyler's gaze cut to the brunette. "I hired *you* for how you look too, you know."

Kathy gestured to the waitress and then pointed to herself. "Beauty and brains, not just beauty. Or at least not just implants."

Tyler made a hissing sound. "Down, kitty." He waved a hand. "Like I said, I'll keep the ones who are competent and get rid of the rest, and let's use those brains of yours to help me think of new ideas. If you can figure out all that crap with the Eyes, you can help me think of a way to make more money." He looked down. "Maybe another Black Sun with a different atmosphere? A new place? An expansion?"

Kathy crossed her arms. "It pains me to say it, but you might be onto something."

"Of course I'm on to something. I'm an expert businessman."

"I don't know if betting on Brownstone counts as being an expert businessman." Kathy rolled her eyes.

Tyler snorted. "I evaluated where to put my money, and the risks. Those risks paid off. That's expertise." He gestured around the bar. "Now I have a bar where cops and crooks both come and don't fuck with each other, and I pick up good information because of that. But it's at its limit, so I need a new place. Just need to stick it halfway across the city or something."

Kathy shrugged. "Like I said, I think you've got the beginnings of a good idea."

"Yeah, I do." Tyler smiled. "This way *I* can win, too."

"Win? Win what?"

Tyler pointed to the front door. "See that door?"

Kathy nodded. "Yeah, what about it?"

"It's a new one. Brownstone destroyed the old one. I'll never be tougher than him, but I can show him who the better businessman is." Tyler grinned. "Yeah, I like where this is going."

---

Trey and his men sat at a table in Jessie Rae's. Ribs and brisket filled platters in front of them as the men gobbled down meat sauced and seasoned to perfection. Many customers had come in for pick-up orders, but the bounty hunters were the only ones eating in.

Lachlan nodded toward the wall with a grin. There were a couple of pictures of Brownstone, but also a couple of pictures of men from the Brownstone Agency.

"I like being famous." Lachlan grinned.

Daryl snorted. "You ain't famous, fool. People know Brownstone, but when they see your picture, they all be like, 'Who the fuck is this? Did he choke on a bone?'"

"They say the same thing about you, bitch."

Daryl shrugged. "Do you even understand any of that Marcus Aurelius we read?"

"Huh?" Lachlan blinked.

The other man slapped his chest. "Worry about yourself, motherfucker, and not any other bitches. That's what the emperor was laying down. You can't control other people. You can only control yourself."

Lachlan frowned and nodded.

Trey stared at the text on his phone, his jaw tight, and a rib halfway in his mouth. "Shit," he mumbled around the rib.

Kevin looked up from the brisket he was devouring. "If you call Jessie Rae's shit, you best be moving to Antarctica, because the big man is gonna kick your ass so hard you'll end up on the moon."

The other bounty hunters nodded their agreement.

Trey shook his head. "Not that. Longshot from an informant just paid off. Wasn't expecting much because we still don't have the kinds of connections here we have in LA, but he's got a line on two level fours. You ever hear of Ben and Claire Harris?"

Lachlan shook his head. Daryl and Kevin shrugged.

"Seriously?" Trey looked at the men. "It's called being proactive, motherfuckers. Try it. Married. People call them the Honeymooner Assassins. They found some weird magical shit on their honeymoon that changed them and made 'em tougher; able to move shit. Telekinesis. It's all cute until you hear how they've used those powers to become professional killers. They've even murdered some FBI and PDA agents."

Daryl whistled. "Damn."

"They ain't supposed to even be in this country right now." Trey frowned. "And they ain't gonna be in Vegas long according to this information. If we're gonna move on them, we've got to do it in the next few hours, or they'll get away."

Lachlan shook his head. "You still recovering from getting hit in the head? Did your healing potion not work? We ain't come up here for no magical bounties. We don't even have our anti-magic gear with us, and not only that, we're running a small team. There ain't no way we're gonna take down two level fours with just the brothers at this table."

Trey furrowed his brow. "I've got my gloves."

Daryl snorted. "Whatever, Brownstone Junior. You tougher now, but that still isn't enough."

Kevin finished his latest rib and set it down. "Why not

just call for reinforcements? Have them bring the gear? Or call the big man and bring him in?"

"Not enough time." Trey shook his head. "And the big man's supposed to be on vacation. We call him begging for help, we're gonna look like little bitches."

"Then what's your plan?" Lachlan asked with a frown. "We charge in there and get ourselves killed?"

"We need local backup." Trey lifted his phone. "And I know just who can provide it."

## CHAPTER SIX

The Brownstone Agency's men filed out of their Expedition into the parking lot of a motel, this time without stun rifles. The Honeymoon Assassins were a dead-or-alive bounty, perhaps unsurprising after their murders of law enforcement officers. If the bounty hunters could take the pair alive they'd score a better payday, but Trey wasn't taking any chances with such dangerous opponents.

Trey looked at the neon sign above the hotel. It was missing half the letters. All the magic and technology in the world, and seedy places somehow always looked run down in the same way. *If we went to some shitty inn on Oriceran, it'd probably look the same.*

A red Ferrari zoomed into the parking lot, its engine nearly silent. It screeched to a halt.

*Electric Ferrari? I know it's good for the planet and shit, but something's wrong when you have a sports car that don't have a nice roar.*

Victoria Stone emerged from the car wearing an even more expensive suit than Trey.

*Why does she always have to show me up like that?*

The pale redhead strolled over to the bounty hunters, her slender hands in her pockets. "Before I go in with you, I want the terms of this little joint operation to be clear."

Trey nodded. "Fine by me."

The witch's gaze cut between Trey and the motel. "I'm not taking twenty percent of the bounty, I'm taking fifty percent."

"What the fuck?" Lachlan shouted. "That ain't fair."

Victoria shrugged. "You can't take those two by yourselves."

"You can't either, bi—"

Trey slapped him upside the head. "Watch your fucking mouth, Lachlan, and show some damned respect."

Victoria raised an eyebrow at Lachlan. "You don't want to get on my bad side."

He glared at her. "Just sayin'."

"Half a bounty is better than no bounty," Trey explained. "And Mr. and Mrs. Harris ain't gonna be around for much longer." He locked eyes with Lachlan. "I need you. You in, or you gonna be a bitch?"

The younger man shrugged. "Yeah. Whatever."

Trey nodded. "Kevin? Daryl?"

The other two men grinned. "This shit's gonna be epic. Let's show them what it means to be a Brownstone bounty hunter."

Trey turned back toward Victoria. "Deal. You get fifty percent, but only because we're in a hurry. Normally, I wouldn't let you do us like that."

He grabbed the gloves from his pockets and slipped them on.

The witch narrowed her eyes and stared at his hands. "Those are new."

Trey grinned. "You understand what they are?"

She gave him a half-smile. "They're magic, that's for sure."

Victoria chuckled. She slipped her hand inside her jacket and pulled out her thin golden wand. "This might be easier than I thought." She grinned. "You might have been able to get me to not agree to fifty percent if I had known about those."

Lachlan frowned. "You do now."

She shrugged. "A contract, verbal or otherwise, is a contract. Just ask Trey how I treat men who disrespect me."

Trey nodded toward the motel. "Now that we've got a witch, maybe they'll do the smart thing. Come on."

The five bounty hunters marched through the parking lot and onto a walkway that took them past several rooms and an algae-filled pool that would probably soon give birth to monsters, from the looks of it.

"You know the nice thing about motels?" Trey asked.

Victoria shook her head. "What?"

"No back doors." Trey grinned.

They arrived at Room 109, the location of the couple according to his informant. The blinds were closed.

Victoria made a few quick movements with her wand. After a bright flash, illuminated glyphs covered her suit, and her eyes glowed bright red.

The bounty hunters all raised their weapons as Trey knocked a few times.

*Hope this shit goes down easy.*

"Who is it?" called a woman from inside.

"Claire and Ben Harris, my name is Trey Garfield, and I'm with the Brownstone Agency. You have valid level four dead-or-alive bounties on you. If you surrender immediately you will not be harmed, but if you resist, we will have to beat your asses down, and your safety will not be assured. Please be aware that not only do we have a major group of badasses out here, but we also have a witch backing us up this fine Vegas evening. Why don't you do the smart thing for all of us?"

Claire laughed on her side. "Do you hear this, honey?"

"I told you someone might come sniffing around, Claire," Ben complained.

Trey adjusted his tie and frowned.

*You fuckers don't know who you're about to screw with.*

He motioned for everyone to back up. They moved a few yards back near a palm tree surrounded by small rocks on the ground.

"Gonna give you about thirty seconds, and then we'll have to do this the hard way," Trey shouted. "This don't have to be no big mess. That's on you."

Claire scoffed. "You think we're coming willingly on a dead-or-alive bounty? They'll almost certainly give us the death penalty, even if you don't kill us."

"At least you have a chance this way."

Claire smirked. "A chance? Honey, what do you think?"

Ben murmured something Trey couldn't make out. A moment later, the door ripped off its hinges and shot forward. Trey jumped to the side, but the slab slammed into Daryl and Kevin, knocking them to the ground with a loud *thud*.

The window exploded a second later, dozens of sharp shards blasting out as if from the twisted shotgun of a giant. Trey's eyes widened as the glass sped toward Lachlan.

Victoria shoved him out of the way. Several shards slammed into her, disappearing in a series of bright flashes. The other shards flew past and embedded deep into the trunk of the palm tree behind them.

A tall blonde woman in a belted blue robe stepped out, followed by a much shorter shaven-headed man in boxers and a wifebeater.

Trey fired once at Claire and Ben, but the bullets dropped to the ground with a *ting* before hitting them. Lachlan emptied his clip from his position on the ground but accomplished nothing more than making a small pile of bullets at Claire's feet.

He was jerked into the air and kicked his feet, Claire's hand slowly rose. She dropped it, and the bounty hunter slammed into the ground with a crunch.

*Fuck, no.*

The woman peered at the fallen bounty hunter and sneered. "Congrats on not dying right away. That makes you tougher than even most of the feds who've come after us."

Victoria twirled her wand in her fingers and didn't say anything.

"Don't worry, witch." Claire smiled. "We'll finish off your little friends first."

Kevin and Daryl groaned, but their eyes weren't open.

Lachlan was breathing, but also unconscious. Trey gritted his teeth. They were alive, which meant their healing potions could take care of their problems, but that left only Victoria and Trey to deal with Claire and Ben.

Trey holstered his pistol. "This still don't have to be a big deal."

Claire laughed. "You're the one putting your gun away." She nodded at her husband. "He thinks that since he has a witch, he can win." She lifted her hand and frowned. "You're not moving."

"Nope," Trey replied with a grin. "What? Your shit don't work on people with magical protection?"

"You both talk too much," Victoria muttered. She pointed her wand, and a golden energy blast shot from the tip and struck Claire. The bounty flew back and slammed against the wall, hissing. She fell to one knee and glared at Victoria.

Her husband growled and thrust out his hands. Hundreds of rocks shot up from the ground to pelt her, disappearing in flash after bright flash against her suit. Victoria stumbled back, the glyphs of her suit dimming.

Several palm fronds ripped off the tree and flew toward Victoria and Trey. The low-velocity plant parts simply bounced off the witch, and Trey batted them out of his face. Claire and Ben sprinted down the walkway toward the parking lot.

Victoria leveled her wand and fired another ball of golden death, narrowly missing the criminals as they turned the corner. "Whatever shield they have doesn't seem to handle magic well. You might have a chance with those gloves."

Trey pointed toward the fleeing bounties. "I'll catch up. Just need to give these guys their potions."

She nodded and rushed after the escaping bounties.

Trey knelt and pulled each man's healing potion out of their jackets, opened their mouths, and poured it down their throats, his heart pounding. They were all still breathing, but it was hard not to remember Shorty.

*I fucked up. I shouldn't have gone after level fours without our anti-magic gear, even with Victoria helping.*

His work finished, Trey stood. Healing potions would take care of their injuries, but it wouldn't wake them up, and he couldn't leave Victoria to take on the bounties alone.

Trey spun and sprinted toward the parking lot. The sounds of shattering glass and wrenching metal filled the air.

"That don't sound good." He hit the corner and turned. Victoria was on one knee near a wall in a pile of glass, blood trailing down the sides of her face. The glyphs on her suit were dim now, and her breathing was labored. A smashed car lay a few feet from her.

Ben was sprawled face-down in the parking lot. Claire stood over him, her arms out.

Another car flew toward Victoria. She tried to roll out of the way as the tons of metal, plastic, and glass sped toward her but screamed as the car pinned her leg. With one final bright flash, the glyphs on her suit disappeared.

Claire glared at Victoria, hatred on her face. "Now you die, witch."

Trey charged toward the bounty. "Yo, forget about me, bitch?"

The blonde spun toward him, her lips curling into a sneer.

Her breathing ragged and her face contorted in pain, Victoria waved her wand. Several golden lines shot toward the car and shoved it backward, freeing her leg. The torn, bloodied, and bent limb was obviously shattered.

Trey ignored her for the moment and continued charging Claire. A motorcycle flew his way. He ducked under it, raising his fist, and yelled as he closed on the bounty. A bumper flew low, and he hurdled the chrome.

*Should have been in the fucking Olympics with these moves. Hope this shit works.*

A few more yards turned into feet, and he barreled into Claire. They crashed to the ground. Claire raised her hand, and a shard of glass flew to it.

"I'll kill you, bounty hunter scum," she snarled, and stabbed Trey, her grip so tight around the glass that it cut her hand.

He winced as the shard pierced his chest, but the spike of pain was far less than he'd expected. Claire stabbed a few more times before he slammed a gloved fist into her face twice. She slumped, unconscious, her hand dropping to the side.

Trey stood up and looked down at his shirt. Bloodstains spread from the locations of the stabs, but when he pulled away his shirt and undershirt to inspect the damage, the wounds were small.

"Good job," Victoria called from behind him.

He turned around. Her suit was shredded in several places, but her wounds were gone. He wasn't surprised. A witch could get healing potions, even if she couldn't make them herself.

Victoria slipped her wand into her jacket holster. "She almost had me there after I took out the husband."

Trey glanced at Ben. He lay in a pool of blood, his eyes open in a death stare.

Distant sirens sang in the night. The police would be there soon.

He rubbed the back of his neck. "Shit, hope our agency insurance pays for some of these cars. If we have to pay directly, we won't clear much on the job."

Victoria smirked. "Next time we should lure the bounties to somewhere we can destroy with a little less concern." She blew out a breath and ran a hand through her short red hair. "Or at least somewhere with fewer cars to throw." She nodded to Trey. "You've got good instincts, by the way. I was right to partner with you on this job."

Trey shook his head. "Nah, it ain't about good instincts. They help, but it's about good training and examples." He held up his hands. "And some nice magical gloves."

The sirens grew closer.

Victoria stared down at Claire. "The point is, it's nice to know there's someone competent backing me up. It's been a continuing problem through my various…careers, you could say. It's been interesting since I've switched over to bounty hunting. It's obvious, for example, that if I had tried to go after this couple by myself, I would have been killed."

"Yeah, that's why we always do teams in the Brownstone Agency." Trey shrugged. "The big man's the only one who goes solo, and even he has his woman with him half the time. She might not be him, but she still kicks ass. Fuck, even his daughter tears shit up."

Victoria smirked. "What a wonderfully destructive family."

Trey laughed. "You don't know the half of it. Just saying, if you want to take on high-end bounties and be sure that someone has your back, maybe you should consider joining the agency. We're recruiting right now, trying to grow it past just me and my boys. You wouldn't be the first new hire. We've taken on a former AET officer and several other new recruits in the last few weeks. What we *don't* have is a badass witch with a good sense of style."

Red and blue lights shone down the road. The police were almost there.

Victoria blew out a breath. "I'll admit I'm interested, but I'm not moving to Los Angeles. I like Las Vegas."

Trey shrugged. "We usually have a Brownstone team in Vegas. You won't always be working with my handsome self, but you *will* have someone to back you up—trained men who have fought everyone from punk-ass bitches to monsters summoned by the Council. I'm sure you heard about them in the news."

"I'll think about it." The witch scratched an eyelid. "And I'll admit there's also a certain appeal about being associated with James Brownstone."

Trey grinned. "I have to run it by the big man, but I doubt he'll say no."

Lachlan, Kevin, and Daryl came around the corner, their guns out.

Daryl looked at the smashed cars. "This shit all over?"

"Yeah," Trey replied, "this shit's all over."

---

Trey didn't bother to call James until the bounty hunters had smoothed things over with the police and returned to the loft above their Vegas office. He hesitated for a moment, wondering if it was a good idea.

*Will Zoe be jealous if I'm working with another hot witch?*

Zoe was more than enough for him. He had no intention of pursuing Victoria, but he wasn't sure his girlfriend would see it that way. He sat on the couch and shook his head.

Women were trouble, magical women even more so.

*Never gonna cheat on her. She's more than enough woman for me. So, if I'm never gonna cheat on her, there ain't no problem. We need magical support, and some of those will end up being hot witches. Just the luck of the draw.*

Trey dialed Brownstone.

"Problem?" James answered, his rumbling voice sounding even deeper over the phone.

"Nah. Why would you think there's a problem?"

"Because it's late. You almost never call me late."

Trey grimaced. "Shit, you're right. Didn't even think. Sorry to bother you on your vacation, big man."

"It's fine."

"And nah, there's no problem." Trey smiled. "Just was finishing up with the level fours I texted you about. Guys got a little banged up but nothing serious."

James grunted. "Good. And the witch?"

"Pretty badass. The bounties dropped cars on her and shit, and she kept going," Trey explained. "We wouldn't have been able to take down the bounties without her. That's why I'm calling. Wanted to talk about her."

"You want to give her more of the money?"

Trey laughed. "Nah, she's already getting half. I brought up with her about maybe joining the agency. She don't want to work in LA, but she's game for Vegas. Figured we could use a witch, but you're the boss. You make the calls."

"I trust you," James replied. "If you think she'll be useful, then let's bring her on. A more permanent presence in Vegas will help, too. Call your aunt and get her started on the hiring process."

"That simple?"

James grunted. "Why the fuck not? We don't need to overthink this shit. If you, Maria, or Royce say something makes sense, I'm gonna listen. Anything else?"

Trey thought that over for a few seconds. "Nah, that was it. Figured this would be a longer conversation. Guess the Brownstone Agency now has its first witch."

# CHAPTER SEVEN

Aiyn leaned back in her seat, keeping her breathing steady as the data flowed. The ocular implant might be transmitting the data directly to her brain, but it was indistinguishable from a holographic display in the real world.

"Damn it, Brownstone, it's like you know." She sucked in a breath.

According to her information, Brownstone had gone from being heavily involved in multiple combat operations to taking on only a handful of bounties in the last month. Not only that, the only significant recent incident involved him defeating some robbers at a pet store in Los Angeles.

*That doesn't even make sense. Why is he wasting time fighting small-time criminals?*

The more Aiyn thought about his behavior, the more bile rose in the back of her throat. The Vax were brutal but predictable in their own way. That was part of their terror, but at least that predictability provided some small hope to those who opposed them.

A subtle Forerunner integrating himself into the target society was the worst-case scenario. Brownstone was not only gaining additional time to adapt to all the weapons and magic on Earth, but he was also learning about their defenses and order of battle. What little chance Earth and Oriceran had of striking back would be minimized if the Vax knew who and where to target upon their arrival.

Aiyn sat up and sighed. No. She needed to push Brownstone more and get him somewhere she could handle him.

"Fine, Brownstone. If you want to pretend to be a bounty hunter, then it's time to take advantage of that."

---

Shay paced back and forth in James' living room. Thomas followed her as if under the impression they were going for a little walk inside instead of outside.

*Damn it, damn it, damn it.*

James looked up from the article he was reading on the different types of magic that might be potentially applied to barbeque and watched Shay for about a half minute.

"What's wrong?" he rumbled.

Shay threw up her hands, and Thomas barked. "I let it get in my head. I thought it'd go away, but it's stuck there."

"What?" James set his phone down.

She stopped and pivoted to face him. "The idea that we're waiting for the other shoe to drop; that we have some sort of luck we need to reset. I've tried to convince myself it's not a big deal, but now I'm thinking about it all the time." She shrugged. "And I'm getting cabin fever."

James blinked. "This isn't a cabin."

Shay rolled her eyes. "You know what I mean." She sighed. "Look, the bedroom fun is great, but, you know, I can't be sore *all* the time."

"I'm not following you."

"We need to stop sitting around. Like I said before, we need to take a job." Shay pointed to him and then herself. "Both of us. Together. It'll reset the luck if there is a problem, but it'll also relax us. We'll get the cabin fever out of us."

James shrugged. "I *am* relaxed. I'm not worried about people coming at me; just think it's a good reason not to start a restaurant. As for jobs, I've had a few people the last few days pushing me to go for some bounties, though."

Shay pursed her lips. "What? You have?"

"Yeah, but none of the jobs are in America. One guy wants me to go to the Australian Outback. Claims there's some sort of monster they need killed. Another guy's begging me to kill a despair bug they found in Hokkaido. Chinese government claims they need me to deal with rogue wizards." James shrugged.

Shay stared at him. "Those all sound perfect. Why didn't you say anything?"

He grunted. "They are all remote as fuck. If this shit's supposed to be about both of us being relaxed, how is shoving my ass on a plane for a huge amount of time gonna relax me? Even supersonic's gonna take a long time if I have to go to China or Australia or some shit. Also, everyone's so pushy. It's rare people contact me directly, and suddenly I get a bunch? What the fuck is up with that?"

Shay scrubbed a hand over her face. "Are you purposely fucking with me right now? Your profile's a lot higher after the Council shit. Of *course* more people are gonna contact you."

"I don't want to fly to Australia." James shrugged. "If I'm still on semi-vacation, then jobs need to be closer. Mexico, maybe. Nothing super-long on a plane."

She sighed. "Okay, fair enough. We don't even need a tomb raid at this point. Let's just go find some level four in Mexico and kick his ass together."

James rubbed his chin and furrowed his brow. After a moment, he stood and headed to his coatrack to grab his jacket. "Let's go, then."

"Go where? Mexico?"

"No." He slipped his coat on. "To the Leanan Sídhe. It's like you suggested before. The Professor might have something. If we're gonna do this shit, I think it should be something that involves artifacts, or you might get cabin fever again in a week."

Shay nodded. "Okay, sure. You're right. Let's go. It's not like we *have* to do this, but it'll get it out of our systems."

"Like I said, I'm relaxed. I'm only doing this because you keep bugging me about it." James chuckled and headed toward the garage.

---

The Professor gave them each a broad smile as Shay finished explaining the situation, including her exact belief in both resetting their luck clock and fighting cabin fever.

She saw no reason to lie to the man. If anything, Smite-Williams knowing more about her reasoning would help with him finding an appropriate assignment.

He sipped his beer and offered them a red-faced smile. "You're in luck, Miz Carson. I've just the thing. Good bounty, and tomb-raid potential."

James grunted, but Shay leaned forward, interest in her eyes.

"I've been sitting on it the last few days," the Professor continued. "Of course, you two came to mind immediately, but I wanted to respect your time off after everything that happened with the Council." He chuckled and let out a sigh of relief. "I've been looking into some of my other contacts, but this makes things far simpler since now I know the job will get done."

James shrugged. "We haven't agreed yet."

"Oh, you will." The Professor's eyes gleamed, but that might have just been the beer. "I'm sure of it."

Shay nodded. "What's the job?"

The Professor took a long pull and finished his beer before continuing, "There's an abandoned oil refinery in northern Alberta. It—"

Shay threw up her hand. "One sec." She turned to James, pleading with her eyes. "You said Mexico was close enough. How about Canada?"

James grunted. "Canada's fine."

She smiled at the Professor. "Please continue."

The older man chuckled and nodded. "As I was saying, an abandoned refinery. It's in a remote area, so it's been ignored for years, but a most unpleasant group called the

Brotherhood of Silence has taken up residence in the complex."

"Who the fuck are they?" James asked.

"Weird cult," Shay explained with a frown. "Have all these fucked-up beliefs about how if they can silence their conscience, they'll transcend God."

James frowned. He had a more practical approach to his religion, but the Brotherhood was aching for a little corrective theology in the form of an ass-kicking.

The Professor nodded. "An apt summary. They aren't terrorists per se, but their moral system tends to lead to them hurting a lot of innocent people. The Canadian Department of Magical Affairs is aware of the group and is considering options including military strikes and partnering with the American PDA, but concern about facing them directly has delayed operations, especially since the group isn't currently attacking anyone."

James frowned. "Wait, why are they letting those fuckers stay there?"

Smite-Williams took a deep breath and shook his head. "Everyone's afraid of running into the next Council, lad. No one wants to send their agents and soldiers to be slaughtered, and many governments have become much more cautious about how they're handling these matters." He beamed a smile at the waitress as she delivered a new beer. "But, the Brotherhood already has a level-five dead-or-alive organizational bounty on them." He shifted his attention to Shay. "And on top of that, they have an artifact I want to get my hands on so I can lock it up far, far away, if not destroy it."

Shay frowned. "And what artifact is that?"

"An ancient Sumerian urn that enhances magical power."

She shrugged. "Tons of those kinds of things around."

The Professor shook his head. "This one is fueled by blood, but not just any blood—only blood taken from conscious and living sacrifices. I, for one, don't want any artifact around that encourages murder."

Shay winced. "I see your point."

James grunted. "You said these fuckers are level five?"

The Professor nodded. "The organization is, lad. Most of the foot soldiers, as it were, aren't that powerful. Physically enhanced through their leader's magic, and without the urn, he wouldn't even be able to do that. So, he is functionally a level five, even if without the urn he'd be less of a threat."

Shay blew out a breath and grinned. She looked at James. "Come on, this sounds perfect. You get to beat some people down who really have it coming for money, and I get to remove some messed-up shit from circulation. We're not even being mercenaries this time, but straight-up helping people. Maybe the Canadians will give us medals." She smirked.

James chuckled. "Yeah, maybe you have a point. Don't want to get rusty. Kicking guys at pet stores doesn't do much to help." His smile faded. "Wait one fucking second. It's in *Canada*."

"Yeah." Shay shrugged. "What about it?"

"Not just Canada, but northern Canada in December. It's gonna be fucking snowing and cold."

The Professor burst out laughing, "No, lad, it's Canada. Nothing but palm trees, coconuts, and sunshine."

James grunted.

"Yeah, snow is kind of a thing in Canada in winter." Shay laughed. "Come on, don't be such a pussy. This shit is perfect. If we do this, I'll stop bothering you about going back to that French place."

James rubbed the back of his neck. "The food there was shit, and they don't give you enough."

"Shit because it wasn't barbeque?" Shay rolled her eyes. "Okay, let me turn this around to make it clear. If we don't do this job, I'm gonna force you to take me there every weekend for the next month."

He groaned. "Fine. Don't like the idea of going to some frozen wasteland, but this Brotherhood and their urn need to be broken."

The Professor clapped his hands together. "Excellent! I'll reach out to my contacts in the Canadian government and make sure there are no crossed wires."

"So much for my vacation," James grumbled.

Shay grinned and rubbed her hands together. "Don't worry, this'll be fun! It's not like the world's on the line or anything this time. It'll practically be a vacation."

---

Aiyn laughed as she read through the data she'd hacked from the Canadian government. Perfect, too perfect.

All her efforts to bait Brownstone to a remote location had failed, and now the monster was willingly walking straight into a textbook area for a trap.

It was hard not to see the hand of Divine Providence leading her. The Vax might not be true demons, but they were dangerous monsters who'd taken many innocent lives for little reason. Some help from above was welcome.

Aiyn nodded to herself. If the Forerunner could be subtle, so could she.

*You won't even see the face of your true killer, Brownstone.*

## CHAPTER EIGHT

Tyler smiled as he gestured broadly at the empty dining room space. "What do you think? We'd have to do some renovation, knock out some walls, but it's workable. They even have a bar already. We can keep the kitchen so we can sell more hot foods. Wings; that kind of thing."

Maria crossed her arms and sighed. "Why are you asking me?"

"You're smart, and you're my girlfriend." Tyler shrugged. "To share something important? I don't know."

"Look, that's sweet and all, but I know how to do police work and kick ass. I don't know crap about business." Maria uncrossed her arms and walked over to a wall. She pointed to a large hole in the baseboard. "I do know *that's* not good. No one wants a bar filled with rats." She frowned. "Well, maybe Willen do, but most don't."

Tyler chuckled and shrugged. "They are easy enough to take care of." He walked over and knelt by the opening.

"That is a big hole. I can't believe they are asking so much for a place that might have an infestation."

Maria surveyed the room, a pensive expression on her face. "Like I was saying, I'm not a businesswoman, and I'm not trying to be a bitch, but are you sure this is a good idea?"

"Why wouldn't it be?" He leaned over and shined a light from his phone into the hole. "Oh, I get it. Don't worry, I'm not stuck on this place. This might not be the best place, but I've got plenty of others to check out. I'm sure I'll find somewhere that works perfectly."

"You don't understand." Maria sighed. "It's not about the location."

Tyler stood and put his phone away. "What, then?"

Maria furrowed her brow. "Let me ask you this: why are you trying to open a second location?"

"I told you already—because I've maxed out the potential of the Black Sun. I need a second location to make more money."

She nodded. "Not going to question the profit motive. I get it; that's your thing. Not going to bust your balls over that, but that leads me on to my next question: do you think opening a second location is the best way to earn more money?"

Tyler shrugged. "I don't run a factory, Maria. I can't just pump out more units. I run a customer-centric business. Starting a second location is one of the best ways to make more money in that kind of business. I've thought about getting into the artifact trade, but that means I'd have to deal with more freaks like the Eyes. Even I have my limits."

Maria ran her finger along the wall and picked up some

dust. She rubbed it between her fingers. "Who are your customers?"

"People who like to drink."

She laughed. "Come on, seriously?"

"I run a bar." Tyler shrugged.

Maria leaned forward to whisper, "The bar's a cover for your real business. You're not a bartender, Tyler. You're an information broker, right? You've told me tons of times you make way more money these days from that than by selling drinks." She pointed toward the kitchen. "More than you'll make from selling shitty wings."

"My wings wouldn't be shitty," Tyler grumped. "I've got a good sauce recipe, or fuck, I'm sure Brownstone could give me a recipe or two. The guy might be mostly good for kicking ass, but he does know his way around meat."

Maria sighed and shook her head. "You're missing my point. I'm kind of surprised because this is about money, and I figured the last thing I'd need to do is spell out shit about money to you." She waved a hand in front of his face. "Your real customers are people who need information about the underworld, not guys who want Brownstone-sauced wings." She tilted her head. "Okay, sure there will be some overlap, but we're talking about your primary customers."

"So what? How does that change anything?" Tyler frowned.

"The point is, you've already got access to the high and low underworld at the Black Sun." Maria shrugged. "It's not like there's some piece of shit who would have paid you for information but decided you were too far away, so he might as well go to his local mom and pop information broker." She gestured around the empty dining room. "Adding a second location will get you some additional money, sure, but probably only on the wings and beer side. You need to think more about how you can expand your information broker career."

Tyler nodded. "I see what you're saying."

Maria barked out a laugh. "I can't believe I'm trying to advise my boyfriend on how to better reach his tentacles into the underworld."

He snorted. "You know you love the danger."

She rolled her eyes. "Whatever you say."

Tyler grinned. "Brownstone-sauced wings. That's *it*."

"Huh?" Maria blinked. "You really think wings are going to help?"

He shook his head. "It's not the wings that are important. It's him—Brownstone. Everything changed with him. I went from being small-time to big-time because of him. He's my good luck charm even if he pisses me off, and when I bet on him, I make money."

"Uh, I still don't think wings are going to be that much of a help. You'd be competing against a lot of places."

Tyler chuckled. "No, no. Fuck the wings. What I'm getting at is I need to stop thinking so much about my own business model and start thinking about how I can invest more in Brownstone or take advantage of *his* business model somehow." He rubbed his chin. "The only question is how?"

Maria sighed. "I'm not following all this, and I joined his agency because I didn't have what it takes to run my own business, but if you want to take advantage of Brownstone and his business, you should match his expansion."

"Match his expansion?"

She nodded. "Adding another place in LA doesn't make much sense. You've already got the information scene covered here, but what about Las Vegas? He almost always has people there now. Hell, I did a rotation a few weeks back myself."

Tyler's eyes widened. "Shit, of course." He chuckled. "I couldn't be there all the time, but I already have someone in mind who would be perfect. It makes much more sense than to expand in LA." He rushed over and threw his arms around Maria, then pulled her in and gave her a deep kiss.

Her eyes widened, and she relaxed into the kiss.

He pulled away, smiling.

Maria blinked a few times. "Didn't realize good business suggestions turned you on so much."

---

James frowned as he looked at his phone.

Shay stood in front of a rack filled with automatic rifles, scratching her cheek. They'd gone to Warehouse Three to gather gear, but she'd been indecisive. He'd learned never to rush a woman trying to pick out her implements of death.

He looked up from his phone. "Already in the 20s where we're going. Lots of snow on the ground."

She pulled down a Steyr and examined it. "I've done jobs in Antarctica, remember? A little snow doesn't bother me. It's not like you've never done a cold-weather job."

James grunted. "Not trying to say we shouldn't go. Just makes me think about the new parka I just bought."

"So you're bitching about it being cold, but you were already prepared?" Shay rolled her eyes.

"Makes life simpler when you're ready." He shrugged, and a grin crept over his face. "I bought it from the same company that makes my gray coats."

Shay groaned. "Of *course* you'd have an ugly parka. You know, it's totally possible to be practical and fashionable at the same time. I looked good even when I was in Antarctica." She snorted. "What's next? You gonna go fight bounties in plaid?"

"Maybe. Don't really give a shit about how things look, just want to make sure I have enough pockets for ammo and equipment."

She set the Steyr back on the rack and pulled down an AK. "This I'm feeling." She turned it over with a smile. "Nothing like a nice, solid, reliable AK. You want to pick out a rifle while we're here, or are we going to swing by Camp Brownstone?"

James shook his head. "Nah. Gonna stick with my .45 and Whispy Doom. I think that'll be enough for this Canadian shit." He frowned. "That reminds me."

"What?"

He held up his phone. "Didn't tell anyone I'd be taking off." He dialed Trey.

Shay nodded and went back to examining her guns.

"Yo, what's up, big man?" Trey answered.

"Canada," James rumbled.

"Yeah, it was still north of us last time I checked." Trey laughed. "What, you punch some fucker through a wall because he was saying it's south?"

James grunted. "No, I'm going to Canada on a job. A level five."

"Oh. You need backup?"

James glanced at his girlfriend. "No. From the sound of it, Shay will be enough."

"Mr. and Mrs. Brownstone kicking ass in the Frozen North." Trey laughed. "Yeah, that works. I'd watch that movie."

James blinked at the phone, warmth spreading through his body. The phrase "Mr. and Mrs. Brownstone" appealed to him far more than he'd expected.

*No. I have to consider Shay's future too, not just what I want.*

"It should be a couple-day thing," James explained. "We know exactly where they are, and it's a dead-or-alive, so I'm thinking we'll focus on the dead part." He grunted. "If they surrender, we'll probably have to wait for the Canadian government. That'll add a day."

"Better bring a space heater," Trey joked. "It's damned cold up there. Colder than a witch's tit."

"Well, you *are* the resident agency expert on witch tits," James replied.

Trey burst out laughing. "Damn, big man! I didn't see that coming. Fuck. I should have known after you won that Bard of Filth shit. You've been waiting to ninja-stab my ass with a burn."

James smiled.

Shay pulled down an RPG from another rack. "Is this too much? Hmm. Maybe."

Trey's laughter died. "Nah, it ain't the Bard of Filth. When I first met you, the only time you said shit was when you were about to beat some motherfucker down, but I've noticed you've been cracking more jokes. I think it's the influence of the big woman on you."

"Big woman? You mean Shay?"

Her head jerked his way, and she narrowed her eyes. "Big woman?"

James shrugged. "Look, Trey, I would never call her that where she can hear you if you value your balls."

Trey snort-laughed. "You're right. Sorry. You enjoy Canada. I'm gonna keep my ass here in Las Vegas where it ain't freezing and eat me some more Jessie Rae's. You're not gonna get any barbeque because all the meat up there is frozen solid. You'll have to survive off those fries they put gravy on."

"Poutine," James explained.

"Damn. Canada really is a foreign country."

# CHAPTER NINE

Tyler smiled as he shifted in his chair behind his office desk. He hadn't been this excited about an idea since the pay-per-view with Brownstone. A few snags aside, that'd been an excellent example of his business acumen.

*I don't care what Maria and Shay said. Brownstone won, and we made money. What's life without a little risk? Nothing more satisfying than making money in a way that doesn't involve* me *getting punched and kicked, though.*

He chuckled. Those bastards hadn't gotten their asses handed to them by Maria.

*That's what you get, assholes.*

A light knock came from the door.

"Come in," Tyler called.

The door opened and Kathy stepped inside, a quizzical look on her face. She looked back and forth as if she expected the Eyes to pop out of a corner.

"You wanted to see me?" she asked. "At least that's what

your text said, but I can't figure out why you couldn't come out and talk to me." She shrugged.

"This is a private conversation, and it requires a certain atmosphere that we can't achieve in the crowded bar." Tyler nodded to the chair in front of his desk. "So sit. We've got a lot to chat about, you and me."

Kathy eyed her boss for a moment before sitting in the chair. She crossed her legs and rested her hands in her lap. "Don't say anything that'll make me think less of you. I might snark a lot, but you have given me reasons to respect you lately. So, with that in mind, what's all this about?"

"Respect? Oh, you'll love this. Money." Tyler smiled. "More specifically, how we can both go about making more of it. Isn't making money what it always comes down to?"

"For you, anyway." Kathy shrugged. "But you still have a few strands of a conscience left, so you won't do something totally over the line, which is probably why you landed a cop girlfriend." She frowned. "Ex-cop girlfriend. Whatever."

Tyler shook a finger at Kathy. "That's the thing. That ex-cop girlfriend has more business skill than I thought. Because of her idea, I'm going to make a lot of money, but this is where you come in. There's only so much money I can make without a little assistance from you, and a good businessman utilizes all his human resources."

"A good necromancer does too." Kathy snickered. "Why do I have a feeling I should run screaming down the streets to get away from you? Maybe I should go ask the Eyes for more help? Maybe he'd look at me with less hungry eyes."

"Very funny." Tyler leaned forward. "It's not a big deal,

and you should be flattered. First, let me explain. I was out scouting locations for a possible Black Sun expansion with Maria."

Kathy nodded. "I'm sure she loved that."

"Yeah, she liked it about as much as you'd expect, but the point is, she gave me a great idea when we were checking places out. Something I hadn't thought of before." Tyler pointed at Kathy. "But I need you for this idea to work."

"Me?" She frowned. "What about me?"

"I'm not going to open a Black Sun expansion in Los Angeles. My business model is info-broker-centric, and there's not as much to be gained by adding another Black Sun here. That's what Maria helped me understand. I'd been thinking I could scale up the business just by opening another place, but that doesn't really work because of what I do."

Kathy frowned. "Then what else are you planning to do? And you still haven't answered how this involves me. If it involves me going back and talking with the Eyes anytime soon, screw that. I need a little bit more time before I have to deal with that…thing again." She shuddered.

"Nah, we can leave that freak in his little soul opium den for a while." Tyler waved a hand dismissively. "No, I'm not opening a new place in LA, because I plan to open a new place somewhere else. Specifically, Vegas."

"Vegas?" Kathy furrowed her brow and looked down. "Why Vegas? Oh, the Brownstone Agency." She looked up. "Is that why? You following your good luck charm to a new city?"

Tyler nodded. "No, I'm following a business opportunity to a new city. The smart play is to go where Brownstone's influence is, and I'm entering a business environment where there's also a certain amount of predictability. Brownstone and his people are going to be in places where there's crime, which means there's a niche for me—or at least my business—to fill." He shrugged. "I offer a product that can be useful for everyone, and they offer me money. Win-win."

Kathy crossed her arms. "The Black Sun also has the protection of the police and is neutral ground, which is one of the reasons it's become so successful. Even without Maria, the LAPD and AET are still upholding that neutrality. Why would Vegas cops care about your new place? They don't know you, and I doubt they'll commit to protecting a place even if you get Maria to call them up and ask them."

"They probably won't." Tyler shrugged. "And I wouldn't ask Maria to do that."

"If it's not neutral ground, it won't be as popular. It'll hurt you from a business perspective."

"I agree," Tyler replied. "But when you can't depend on the government, you depend on private services. That's the American way."

Kathy shook her head. "Having security isn't good enough. People need to fear the group enforcing the neutrality. Random hired thugs aren't going to have the power of the police behind them."

Tyler nodded. "Exactly, which is why I'm going to get the Brownstone Agency folks to agree to enforce the neutrality of the new place."

"Are you serious?" Kathy laughed. "Why would he? Just because he's done some business deals with you doesn't mean he's going to agree to something like that."

Tyler shrugged. "Don't worry, I'll figure out something. Free drinks for his guys, free info when they're in town, that kind of shit. Business is ultimately about negotiation. You have to make something worth someone else's while, and I'll make it worth his while. You know how it goes with Brownstone. His name is enough anymore to get people to back down, and anyone he targets goes down, so anyone who has a beef with him won't last long enough to threaten me or my place."

Kathy sighed. "Okay, let's assume you convince Brownstone and his people to protect your neutrality. Where do I fit in?"

Tyler smiled. "Isn't it obvious? I need someone to run the place. I can't drive back and forth every day between Vegas and LA. I've got a lot of ties to Los Angeles, but we both know that you don't. You've proven you're not just a pretty face, and I think you'd be a good choice to lead an expansion in Las Vegas. You'd manage the bar and the info business, and I would front the cost of the place and some other things. You're out from underneath my shadow, so you can build up your own influence, but I still profit and don't even have to do that much. Again, win-win."

Kathy stared at him for a moment before frowning and nodding. "I got a decent chunk of change from Brownstone for helping him with He Who Hunts, you know. What's to stop me from moving to Las Vegas and opening up my own place and getting rid of the middleman here? If it's such a good idea, why shouldn't I steal it?"

"Nice, very nice." Tyler shook his finger and grinned. "You act like you care less about money than I do, but you've got the fire in the end. That's exactly how you *should* be thinking, but before we start talking about any other details, I just want to be clear. Would you be willing to move to Vegas? If you aren't, then I have to figure out how to find someone else I might trust."

It might be dangerous to admit he trusted Kathy, but extending trust was part of building a business, as Brownstone had already proven with his agency.

Kathy shrugged. "Why not? You're right. I'm newer to LA. I don't have a boyfriend or family or anything here. Not even a pet. It's just a place I ended up. So, yeah, I guess I *am* interested, but I don't want to be your employee anymore. I'm willing to front money for this to ensure that. Maybe I don't want to do it on my own, but I don't want to have you call all the shots, either. After going through that shit with the Eyes, I feel like I deserve more."

"How about we both do it, then?" Tyler steepled his fingers, adopting his best Bond villain smile, confidence radiating from his face. "We both kick in money, and I still get a percentage. We also cooperate, share tips both ways; that way we're both benefiting and building our brands. I also have contacts in Vegas who can help kickstart your position there." He leaned back. "Yeah, you could go there and grab your own place, but without me opening doors, it's going to be a lot harder for you to get established. So, if you don't want to be my employee, why not agree to be my partner?"

"Partners? And you're willing to accept that?" Kathy

eyed him with suspicion. "The man who didn't even want waitresses because they cost him money?"

"I've evolved due to changing market conditions. I also used to hate Brownstone's ass and hope he got killed, but he's made me money, and now I've partnered with him." Tyler shrugged. "I'm interested in any deal that can make me money, and partnering with you can make me money for very little effort other than an initial investment. I'm tired of being short-sighted when I could be a little more rational and make a shitload more money."

"Still seems generous for you. You can't blame me for being suspicious."

Tyler laughed. "Generous? The only reason I'm willing to talk about being a partner is that you're willing to kick in some of your own money. That means I don't have to invest as much upfront, and I'll be turning a profit a lot sooner." He leaned back in his chair with a smirk. "And in the end, it all comes down to money. This isn't about you being hot or smart or brave or any shit like that. Those are just things you have that make you useful for the position."

"How nice." Kathy snorted.

"It's simple. I need your help to make me money, so I'm cutting you in. I'm not here to blow smoke up your ass about it. If you want to make money, we can do this. If not, I'll move on."

"Huh." Kathy stared at him in silence.

Tyler waited, thinking about all the possibilities and ways to convince Brownstone to expand into other cities so he could send other people there for similar arrangements. A brief vision of an entire national network of information brokers funneling cash and info into his pocket filled his mind. That thought finally brought a frown.

*I got lucky with Kathy. It'll be awhile before I find another person like her I can trust not to fuck up.*

Kathy shrugged. "Okay, I'm in. What can I say? It's a good idea."

"Excellent." Tyler extended his hand. "I'm happy to make money with you, partner."

She took his hand and gave it a firm shake.

---

James glanced around the busy boarding gate. Dozens of people sat in the plastic chairs that filled the area. Most people stared at their phones, but three men spoke in hushed tones near the window. The slender mid-range supersonic passenger plane was already parked outside the gate.

*At least I won't have to be on the damned plane for long.*

A plane at a nearby gate slowly backed up and turned to taxi to the runway.

Magic might have returned to the world, but most humans—or aliens pretending to be humans—still depended on an iteration of the aircraft that had filled the skies for decades.

*Huh. Will things be different for Alison when she's my age? We've got shit like Currus now. Maybe the world will be a lot fancier when technology and magic are mixed more.*

*What about my amulet? Is that magic or technology? Like Currus cars?*

James looked around, taking in the crowds sitting and

walking around him. Shay had wandered off to the bathroom, but they had plenty of time before boarding began, so he wasn't worried. They'd arrived early to do all the bounty hunter paperwork for their equipment, but he'd flown out of LAX often enough that the Customs agents could go through all the inspections and procedures swiftly.

He nodded to himself, a sliver of excitement building at the idea of the trip. Shay had been right. While he wasn't thrilled about flying into snowy Alberta from Los Angeles, the idea of taking down scumbags had its appeal. It would also be a good test of Thomas' ability to handle being away from his new owner.

He wasn't that worried. Charlyce was watching the dog, but he seemed fine with the idea of James taking off.

*Shouldn't be surprised. He was on the streets when I found him.*

One of the three men speaking in hushed tones glanced James' way. One of his friends frowned at him and muttered something.

James grunted and checked for Shay again. Maybe she'd stopped for a bagel after the bathroom. He spared a look at the three men. They had obviously been watching him.

Something was off. Their shoulders were too tense, their frowns too deep. A man couldn't be a bounty hunter for his entire adult life and not spot a troublemaker in a crowd.

*Not my problem. They don't have bounties. Or do they? Wouldn't have enough time to get them processed before taking off, though. Your lucky day, assholes. Still...*

James frowned and pulled out his phone, bringing up

his bounty hunting app. He tapped the option for facial recognition and held his phone up to take a picture of the men.

They all stared at him, deep scowls on their faces.

He waited for the picture to process and match against bounties in the Los Angeles and Calgary areas.

**NO MATCHES BASED ON SELECTED PARAMETERS.**

If they weren't local or Calgary bounties, he didn't give a shit. He wasn't going to fly somewhere else for small-fry bounties.

One of the men marched over to him. "Hey, what was that about?"

James looked up at him. "What?"

"You just took our picture, didn't you?"

He shrugged. "Problem?"

The man glared at James. "You can't just take someone's picture in public."

James frowned. "Pretty sure you can, actually. At least in the States. Don't know about Canada." He nodded. "They *are* tight about it in Japan, though. I remember hearing that on my trip there. But I don't take a lot of pictures."

The men's nostrils flared. "Then why did you take *our* picture?"

James shrugged. "So I could match you against wanted bounty databases, but you weren't in any that I care about."

The man swallowed. "You are him, aren't you? James Brownstone. The Scourge of Harriken. The Granite Ghost."

"James Brownstone?" echoed another passenger nearby.

Several people murmured and looked his way. His name apparently carried more weight than his appearance.

The bounty hunter stood with a grunt. "Yeah, I'm James Brownstone." He narrowed his eyes. "You might not be bounties, but you look shifty as hell. Whatever you fucks are thinking about doing, don't. This is supposed to be a fun trip for my girlfriend and me. I already hate flying, and I don't need anything else to make my trip unpleasant. Do I make myself clear?"

The man's eyes widened. He swallowed and looked back at his friends. After he hurried back over to them, all three men picked up their carry-ons and walked away from the boarding area.

James crossed his arms. The entire crowd around him continued to murmur and whisper amongst themselves, occasionally pointing at him.

The trio turned a corner as Shay reappeared from the opposite side of the boarding area. She made her way to James, blueberry muffin in hand.

She held up the muffin with a smile. "I figured you wouldn't want one, considering the only sweet things you care about are barbeque sauces."

James grunted. "I'm good."

Shay leaned in to whisper into his ear, "I didn't want to tell you because I wanted to keep things relaxed and I was going to handle it on my own, but maybe seeing you scared them off."

"Tell me what?"

"Oh, just recognized three terrorists. Saw a thing on them on the dark web the other day." Shay took a bite out of her muffin and swallowed. "Wasn't worried, but didn't want you punching them through a window and depressurizing the plane, so I figured I'd take care of it while we were still on the ground. That and go to the bathroom and get a muffin."

"They got pissy because I was taking pictures of them." James glanced toward the corner.

A chime sounded over the PA system.

"All passengers waiting to board the ToddAir Flight 2327 to Calgary, your flight has been delayed for mechanical inspection. We're sorry for this inconvenience, and we thank you for choosing ToddAir."

Groans and angry mutters filled the boarding area.

Shay's phone rang, and she pulled it out with her free hand. "Yes? Okay. Okay. Sure. Thanks, Peyton." She slipped the phone back into her pocket. "I had him place an anonymous call to the airport police about the terrorists," she whispered. "Airport cops already caught them, but I'm guessing they want to inspect the plane before we take off."

James grunted. "Those fuckers *still* managed to screw with our flight. Let's go get something to eat at that steakhouse we passed, then. And, just a reminder, I know how to beat someone down without smacking them through a window."

Her mouth full of muffin, Shay shrugged. "Sometimes you do," she muttered around her food.

---

Aiyn sighed and stared down at the ocean through her living room window. Her first gambit had failed, but the damned fools had been supposed to engage Brownstone once he'd landed in Canada, not eye him in an airport. It was fortunate they had no direct connection to her. They'd been contacted and paid their TrollCoin anonymously.

*It had been a mistake to use such humans. I can't rely on that kind of scum. If things had gotten out of hand, someone innocent might have gotten hurt.*

The Shepherd frowned. She had few choices. If her superiors wouldn't send reinforcements or authorize her personal engagement, she'd have to rely on disposable tools. Brownstone would hurt anyone who came after him, so it was imperative she manipulate the situation to avoid sending honorable law enforcement or military forces after him unless she were certain they would win, but expending criminals who preyed on their own people didn't bother her.

*It's a punishment for them as well as the damned Vax.*

Aiyn shook her head. Her hands twitched with the urge to grab her weapons and confront Brownstone directly. She could taste the joy of watching the monster taking its last breath. The lack of advanced technology on Earth meant the Forerunner was probably better adapted to magic than Alliance weaponry.

"No," she whispered. "I've been handed this Alberta opportunity. I'll use it, and in my next report, I'll tell my superiors about how Brownstone was killed by local magical creatures."

She chuckled. By the time the lie came out, would they even care?

Besides, a monster killing a monster? Pure poetry.

# CHAPTER TEN

Heather tapped away at her keyboard, looking at her two monitors alternately. She didn't like what she was seeing on the forecast. James and Shay could handle themselves fine regardless of weather, but she and Peyton couldn't back them up with drones in bad weather. The refinery should have been a perfect scenario where the hackers could watch James and Shay's backs.

*Damn it. Need some remote-controlled snowmobile drones or something. The military probably has something like that. Then again, how often does James end up in snow country? Not sure about Shay, but she has been to Canada and Antarctica before from what Peyton said.*

"Maybe we'll get lucky, and the blizzard will miss them," Heather mumbled, and shook her head.

An alert popped up, and Heather narrowed her eyes. "What's this?"

Her various bots, spiders and tripwires spread around the internet helped warn her if anyone was looking too closely into her or James. It'd taken her a long time to refine the algorithms to make sure that not every search query from random Brownstone fans would trigger an alarm, especially after her embarrassing first steps taught her an important lesson: there were a lot of thirsty women and men out there on the internet who wanted themselves a little of James Brownstone.

Heather frowned as she looked through log entries and examined some of the data. Whoever she'd caught snooping around definitely wasn't a random fanboy or fangirl asking, "Is Brownstone married?" or "What is Brownstone's favorite type of woman?" or "What's Brownstone's favorite type of man?"

No, this was a directed search by someone or something very familiar with communications technology programming and the modern internet backbone. In other words a professional.

She sighed. This was hardly the first time she'd run into this sort of thing, but the timing was unfortunate, if only because her boss was going to such a remote location where she might not be able to back him up.

*What am I worried about? He's got Shay with him. Those two took out an entire building filled with Harriken. He'll be fine, and whoever is doing this probably isn't magical if they're relying on hacking. That means James and Shay can deal with them the old-fashioned way if they show up.*

Heather submitted some of the recovered data to a few analysis scripts she'd written. Whoever was tripping her alarms had been trying to trace James' phone's exact location, among other things. They were hiding behind a maze of proxy servers, again pointing to a professional. The pattern of proxy servers, along with a few other minor details, confused her. Some of it seemed high-level and professional, and some of it seemed random and scattershot. She also didn't understand the significance of some of the redundant routing or the meaning of certain packets that had been sent. She'd never seen anything like it.

*Something's off about this even if this* is *obviously the work of a pro, but I still spotted it. That means whoever they are, they aren't way above me. Unless I was meant to find them? But why? Shit, I just need to tell him and let* him *worry about it.*

Heather dialed James. Forewarned was forearmed.

"Hello," he rumbled.

"I just thought you should know someone's trying to pay very, very close attention to your exact location," Heather explained. "Someone who knows what they are doing. The timing is definitely related to your trip, so you should assume that when you arrive in Canada, someone will be watching you get off that plane and maybe following you to the refinery."

"Thought so." James grunted. "I was expecting this shit."

"You were?"

"Yeah." James muttered something under his breath. "Probably Canadian intelligence trying to keep an eye on me because I tend to get…loud on jobs. I've got a few people in the American government on my side, but no one like that in Canada."

Heather smirked. "'Get loud?' That's one way to describe it. Should I try to block them?"

"The Professor said he contacted them, but there's no

reason to let them do whatever the fuck they want. You do what you can. It's not like they're going to do anything to me even if I blow up an abandoned refinery because this job is far away from anyone who shouldn't be hurt. It's like the Council—I can beat down who I need to without worrying about shit."

"Okay." Heather chuckled. "I'll block their asses."

"I've got to go," James explained. "Got another call. Busy all of a sudden. Not sure why Mike is calling me, though."

Heather tried to place the name but failed. "Mike?"

"Owner of Jessie Rae's. Maybe there's a competition he wants me to enter."

"It's hard being popular."

The bounty hunter snorted. "Maybe not hard, but complicated. Talk to you soon."

---

Trey and his boys, along with Victoria, sat around the dining room table in the loft thumbing through bounties.

*Damn. I miss having Auntie Charlyce come over here with us and cook, but she's too fucking busy down in LA.*

He glanced at the pale redheaded witch, who stared at her phone with narrowed eyes. Even if Victoria wasn't an official member of the agency yet, it made sense to work with her on new bounties so everyone could get used to each other. The bounty hunters might have trained to fight against magic, but they hadn't trained much with active magical support.

*Will Maria know how to use her?*

Not only did Victoria wield impressive magic, but she

was also a hardass in a different way than Maria. It'd take a while to get used to her personality, but at least she didn't seem to have a problem with them cussing. Smooth Trey might be an option, but most of his boys didn't have a smooth mode.

*Then again, kind of doubt we'll run into someone in this business who can't stand to hear a few "motherfuckers."*

"I think we should just hit up a mess of level twos," Kevin suggested. "They'll be easy. We can nail a lot of them in a row and save the tougher ones for later. A lot of these assholes are itching to be beaten down, thinking they're all big shit. We'll show them who *is* big shit."

Lachlan and Daryl nodded.

Victoria pursed her lips. "Maybe. Don't want anyone running if there's a big sweep, but I doubt any level fours will run just because level ones and twos go down."

Trey shrugged. "Manuel's on his way with the anti-magic gear, and I don't want to move on any more level fours without that anyway. That shit was too close. If we're all geared up, chances of getting hurt are less."

"Fair enough, although I won't let the next few surprise me with a car like that." The witch shrugged and returned to looking through bounties on her phone.

Trey watched her for a moment for any hint of anger, but her expression appeared more focused than annoyed. He'd seen her quit a job over disrespect, and he wanted to make sure she understood that he respected her abilities but didn't want to risk people's lives from arrogance.

His phone rang with a call from James, forcing his attention away from the witch.

"What's up, big man?" Trey answered. "We're in Sin City preparing to beat down sinners, and there's so many."

"I need you to do me a favor," James rumbled, dark menace underlying his words. "It involves Vegas and a beat-down."

Trey pulled the phone back to stare at it for a second with a frown.

*What the fuck? Big man sounds pissed. He always kind of sounds pissed, but he sounds kick-someone-through-the-wall pissed.*

"Sure, what do you need?" Trey replied. "We're not rolling back home anytime soon. Got plenty of time to deliver Brownstone justice to whoever be needing it."

"Go to Jessie Rae's. Mike needs help," James growled. "Someone made a big mistake. His place was robbed."

Trey shot out of his seat. "*Motherfuckers*!"

"Exactly." James let out an even lower growl. "Do what you can, but keep things going with the other bounties. The police are still depending on us, but I consider robbing Jessie Rae's a personal matter. It needs to be handled."

"It's not a problem, big man. I'll personally make sure it's taken care of." Trey pinched the bridge of his nose. "Do you want to be here when it goes down?"

"Yes, unless you find out the fucker is going to skip town," James replied. "Make sure he doesn't get away, though. We can't have criminals fucking with Jessie Rae's. They need to understand that place is under our protection."

"It ain't no big thing. I'll find the fuckers that did this and make them understand why they don't fuck with barbeque. Talk to you soon."

James' only response was an angry grunt.

Trey hung up the phone and shook his head before looking around the table. Everyone stared at him expectantly.

"Some dumb motherfucker robbed Jessie Rae's," Trey explained.

The other men frowned, muttering dark things centered around improbable anatomical rearrangements. Victoria eyed them but said nothing.

Lachlan set his phone down and curled his hands into fists. "We getting involved?"

Trey took a few cleansing breaths to calm his pounding heart. "Here's how we're gonna work it. Big man still wants the show to go on, so I'm gonna go chat with Mike about this shit, and the rest of you can take out every level-two motherfucker you can get your hands on in the meantime. Three of you plus Victoria should make that shit easy, but remember how it goes. Sometimes they surprise you." He smirked at the witch. "I remember when what was supposed to be a simple bounty turned into a showdown with a witch."

She smirked back at him.

Trey marched over to the coat rack by the front door. "And text me when Manuel gets in."

---

Forty-five minutes later, Trey stood behind Jessie Rae's eyeing the charred hole in the back door where a lock used to be.

"Even though the cops have already checked it out,"

Mike explained, "I didn't want to replace it until James had a look at it, but you're fine, too."

Trey narrowed his eyes and squatted by the hole. "This ain't your standard-issue bitch-ass thief. Either someone used some real fancy shit or magic." He rubbed his chin. "That's a good thing, though."

Mike frowned. "A good thing?"

Trey stood. "Narrows it down. Lots of punk-ass bitches with crowbars and guns, not as many with magic. Anything else you think might be helpful?"

Mike sighed and shook his head. "Other than the pictures I sent you, I don't know much. The cameras were fine when the asshole stepped up to the back door, and suddenly there was static. The static cleared and the hole was there, and he went inside. Caught him on camera coming in and out several times."

The thief in the pictures looked young, probably in his twenties, and had a fit build, but there was nothing all that special about him with his jeans and gray T-shirt. He reminded Trey of a guy from his neighborhood he didn't like, Rudy, but it was mostly just some similarities in the face. Rudy's game had been drug dealing, not theft.

*Bitch probably would have stolen from Jessie Rae's. Fuck you, Rudy, and fuck you, thief bitch. You've got Trey Garfield coming for you. Me and the big man are gonna knock on your door and ruin your day. How do you like that?*

Mike glared at the hole. "I don't understand. Why would someone who can use magic rob *me*? They can use damned *magic*."

"You'd be surprised at the shit I've seen in this job." Trey shook his head. "Powers don't always mean shit when it comes to making a living. And scum are scum, magic or otherwise. What did the police say?"

"They're trying their best, but it's not like I'm the only guy to get robbed in Vegas lately." Mike shrugged. "Underpaid and overworked. I gave them the pictures and camera footage and they ran facial recognition, but they said the guy's not in any local or national police databases. Doesn't have a driver's license, either. They couldn't find any DNA or fingerprints, and they're not going to bring in magical forensics for a restaurant robbery."

Trey snorted. "Just because this thief ain't in some databases and has a few magic tricks don't mean he's gonna get away with it. I guaran-fucking-tee you that on behalf of the Brownstone Agency. We can call on people the 5-0 can't. We'll find out who this guy is and track his ass down."

Mike shook his head. "He cleaned out the register and stole a TV, but that's not the worst part. He stole several competition trophies and plaques I had on display. The asshole made several trips. It's not like they're worth a lot if you sold them, but those mean a lot to me. They're part of this restaurant. Part of my family's legacy."

"Don't you worry, Mike." Trey cracked his knuckles. "The only reason the big man ain't here tracking this bitch-ass down himself is that he's got to beat down some magic cult motherfuckers, but I ain't leaving Vegas until I find the guy, and then we're gonna have a very loud and one-way conversation about proper respect." He held up a hand. "And to make this clear. This is pure *pro bono*, you know what I'm saying? This ain't just about thieves. This is about protecting barbeque and making people understand they don't disrespect your restaurant."

"Thanks, Trey. I appreciate it."

Trey smiled. "And we appreciate all the fine barbeque you've fed us."

## CHAPTER ELEVEN

James sat with his arms crossed beside Shay in the small Customs office. The Canadian Customs agent gave him a tight smile every few minutes as he skimmed through the information on the tablet in front of him, occasionally nodding or mumbling something to himself.

The bounty hunter kept his breaths even and slow. He was already pissed about someone screwing with Jessie Rae's, and now the Customs agents had kept him in processing at the Calgary International Airport for an hour. It was usually in and out.

*Maybe Shay was onto something about bad luck. How often do I need to kick ass to make sure I don't have any?*

The Customs agent smacked his lips. "Mr. Brownstone, you've brought quite the impressive arsenal up north, eh?"

James frowned. He hadn't even brought any explosives. Shay hadn't either. It wasn't that much of an arsenal.

"I'm a class-six bounty hunter going after a level-five bounty." He shrugged. "It's not like I can just ask them to surrender. I don't understand. I precleared all this shi… stuff through normal channels. I've flown this kind of thing into Canada on jobs before, and it hasn't taken this long."

*Maybe the Customs guys are bigger dicks when it's colder. Can't blame them, but don't want to sit in the airport all day.*

Shay sat there with a blank expression on her face.

The Customs officer tapped his fingers on his desk next to his tablet. "Yes, Mr. Brownstone, I see that you have brought such weapons and equipment into the country before according to your records, but I also have some notes in this file that suggests you shouldn't be authorized to bring this level of weaponry into Canada. Now, I get that you're a bounty hunter, so it's not like we're going to charge you with smuggling or anything, but this may be a violation of our import laws."

James grunted. "You are fu…you're kidding me."

The other man shook his head, a broad smile plastered on his face. At least he was pleasant while he was screwing James. "Here's what we're going to do, Mr. Brownstone. We're going to have to keep all these items for the moment. You know, impound them. But don't worry, you won't be arrested. You're free to go while we work all this out. As is Miss Carson."

Shay snorted but said nothing.

"We won't be arrested?" James gritted his teeth. "How nice of you."

Shay reached over to pat James' hand and smile at him.

*Don't worry, I'm not going to kick this guy through a window, Shay. Yet.*

The Customs agent nodded. "Yes. No arrests. Not a bad

deal considering you came in with a bunch of illegal weapons, eh? If you want to appeal, feel free to go to the website and file the appropriate forms, but for now, you're free to go. I hope you enjoy Calgary and the rest of Alberta."

Shay tugged at his arm. "Let's go, James. There's nothing we can do for now."

He stood, working his jaw and resisting the urge to smash the smiling man's tablet over his head. He turned and threw open the door and stomped out, Shay close behind.

They emerged from the waiting room and moved into a nearby hallway leading back to the main airport, James' feet pounding the entire way. He glowered at everyone and everything, and several people shrank under his gaze. The minutes passed in silence as the pair made their way toward the rental car counters.

Shay leaned toward him. "This is why smuggling's still handy," she whispered. "Sometimes when you do things the right way, you still get fucked."

James shrugged. "I don't get it. I almost never have problems, and even when I do, they don't impound all my shit. It's just a few extra minutes or whatever. It's been years since I've had this kind of problem." He frowned. "I shouldn't have blown Heather off. She was on to something."

"What do you mean? About someone tracking you?"

He sighed. "The Professor must not have the influence up here he thinks."

Shay nodded. "So you think someone in the Canadian government is purposely fucking with you?"

"Don't know. Maybe. Somebody is." James shrugged.

They turned at an intersection. The density of nearby people increased.

Shay sighed. "That would explain it. At least they know enough not to try and lock us up, and you still have your amulet, so you have the ultimate weapon if you need it."

James shook his head. "This is bullshit." He frowned. "And I'm not relaxed. I was fine and relaxed in LA, and now I'm pissed off."

She laughed quietly. "Yeah, I get that, James. Bureaucracy—it's the one enemy you can't easily kill. We've got a few options, as I see it."

They turned again, passing the sea of humanity flowing past them as they closed on the rental car counters.

"What options?" James asked.

Shay held up one finger. "First, we can just ignore the lack of gear. We can go buy some additional coats and shit, and I can poke around and find someone willing to provide us with more useful offensive toys. There's always someone." She held up a second finger. "Or we can go directly to the refinery, and you do your thing with Whispy Doom, and I hope I can find something on one of their bodies."

James grunted. "We're not going there unarmed. I might not be able to get close enough, and Whispy's too damned unreliable."

"Okay, glad we agree on that." Shay nodded. "Plus, for one thing, they have my Masamune, and we might need that bad boy since we're dealing with magic. Next time I'm just smuggling it in. Anyway, that leaves us with our last major option."

"Which is what?"

"Taking advantage of your fame and influence." Shay smiled. "You forget who you are a lot."

James shrugged. "That guy knew who I was, but he didn't give two fucks. Fame's not gonna get my weapons back from Customs."

"He might have known who you are, but he doesn't know who you know." Shay shook her head. "Pull a few strings—maybe Senator Johnston. If not him, then we should consider Heather or Peyton doing something."

James furrowed his brow. "Don't want them messing around with stuff when it looks like someone else already is. The fewer people who know we have them, the better."

"Senator Johnston it is. He owes us."

James pulled out his phone. "He might tell me to fuck off too. He's a politician. He might already be planning to sell me out as part of his reelection campaign."

Shay snorted. "Doesn't hurt to try."

---

"That is mighty suspicious, son," Senator Johnston commented over the phone. "Though I suspect this is petty bullshit rather than conspiracy. I'll contact some people in the Canadian government, but it is ultimately a foreign country. This might take a few hours, even with my influence."

James grunted. "But you think you can get our gear?"

"Nothing's certain in this world except death and taxes, but I'm on good terms with a lot of people up there. I suggest you relax in the meantime. I'll call you when I have news."

"Thanks." James ended the call and looked at Shay. "He says he'll see what he can do, but it'll take a while."

She shrugged. "It's still pretty early in the day, and it's only two hours to the site. So even if it takes him a few hours, we should be able to still hit the place with daylight on our side."

James shook his head. "Next time I'm sticking to the States when it's supposed to be a relaxing job."

Shay laughed. "Fair enough. Let's go pick up the rental."

---

The older man behind the counter at the rental car company passed the key fob over. "Here you go. One Jeep Ultra Wrangler, red, gasoline engine." He sniffed disdainfully and handed a tablet to James. "You requested maximum insurance. Please review this document, sir."

James slipped the fob into his pocket and started reading the document. After a couple of minutes, he frowned and looked up. "This is the maximum package?"

The employee nodded. "Yes, sir. Is that going to be a problem? Do you anticipate severe damage to the vehicle?"

"I just like to be prepared, and I'm used to different insurance packages in California." James shrugged.

The other man narrowed his eyes. "I see. Well, I encourage you to be careful, and you won't have any trouble. Have a nice day, and enjoy your visit to Calgary."

James turned and walked over to the waiting Shay.

She chuckled. "Maybe I should just start shipping cars

from my warehouse to job locations, so you don't have to go through all this." She smirked. "Not that I have fancy insurance for when you wreck them."

James frowned. "It's fine. You never know what's going to happen, but now I'm even more annoyed. It's like everyone decided to piss on me on the same day." He pulled out his phone. "Time to prove Trey wrong."

Shay arched a brow. "Prove Trey wrong about what?"

James typed in a search query of "best barbeque in Calgary" and waited for the results to pop up. "About Canadian barbeque."

Shay groaned. "I should have known."

---

James patted his stomach and slipped into the driver's seat of the Jeep. "Damn. I have to say the Canadians are putting up a good fight with that kind of meat." He smiled at the fenced-off long table and massive white letters above the building.

HAYDEN BLOCK SMOKE & WHISKEY.

"That *was* straight Texas-style, though," he rumbled.

"Alberta's kind of like the Texas of Canada, so that fits." Shay flicked a wrist after settling into her seat. "It was pretty good, I guess. For barbeque."

James shook his head. "Something's wrong with your mouth for you to say things like that."

She smirked. "That wasn't what you were saying the other night."

He grunted and looked away. Participating in the Bard

of Filth competition didn't mean he was fine with every dirty joke now, just that he understood them better.

"Anyway," James mumbled, "the senator's text said everything should be taken care of, and to go pick up our gear. He said he wasn't sure why they'd screwed with us, but it'd been indicated to him that it'd come up from someone higher up."

Shay nodded, a slight frown on her face. "Still wondering if we should wait a day."

James started the Jeep and pulled into the street. "Why? After all this frustrating shit, I want to get to the ass-kicking part."

"But there's that storm system moving in." Shay shrugged.

James grunted. "I brought the parka, so who gives a shit if it snows? It's annoying and cold, but we're already here, so I don't see the problem."

"I'm just saying our visibility will be reduced by a blizzard." Shay pointed to her eyes. "I only brought one pair of AR goggles. Can't kill what you can't see."

James grunted. "I'll be fine. I want to get this shit done sooner than later."

"Yeah, so much for relaxing." Shay rubbed the back of her neck. "It sounded like a great idea at the time. But the more I think about it, the Brotherhood will be just as handicapped as we are."

A feral grin appeared on James' face. "Besides, I kind of like the idea of hunting them in the snow. It's like I'm a fucking Yeti or something."

"Wendigo," Shay responded.

"'Wendigo?'" James echoed.

Shay nodded. "Cannibal spirit of the North. Yetis are more a Himalayan thing. Don't know if Wendigos are real, but considering half the shit I've run into, I wouldn't count them out." She laughed. "Anyway, you're looking forward to a blizzard so you can run around hunting people like a monster?"

"If I have to be in the cold and deal with snow, might as well have fun doing it." James shrugged.

"Fine. Let's go make you a Wendigo." Shay shook a finger at him. "But no eating anyone. I have to kiss that mouth."

James shrugged. "Don't have any barbeque sauce with me anyway."

# CHAPTER TWELVE

The Jeep's wipers swished back and forth, pushing the accumulating snow off to either side of the windshield. The snowfall had picked up in the last half hour, the dense flakes coating the highway. The wind tried to push the Jeep, but James' steady hands kept his vehicle straight. The thick clouds choking the sky made it far darker than a person might expect for the afternoon.

James glanced in his rearview mirror and rearview camera at a trio of SUVs in the distance behind them. "You see what I see?"

Shay nodded. "Yeah. In the city they could at least pretend to not be following us, and even when we pulled out of Calgary, maybe they could be going the same way, but come on, we've switched to another highway, and we're almost to the turnoff to an abandoned refinery in the middle of nowhere." She rolled her eyes. "They could at least have been subtle. This does let us know one thing, though."

"What's that?"

She looked over her shoulder out the back window. "They aren't Brotherhood. If they were and knew we were coming, they would have gone ahead to ambush us later rather than follow us."

James grunted. "So, some other assholes? Canadian government?"

Shay shook her head. "Nah, it doesn't make sense for them to follow you so closely. They were probably behind screwing with us at the airport, but if they wanted to keep screwing with you, it would have been then. They know your reputation." She sighed. "Someone else, I'm betting. Maybe the terrorists you scared off had buddies already up here, and they called ahead and want a little payback."

He accelerated despite the buffeting winds. "Not interested in random fuckers. Probably won't even get paid for killing them. Nothing but a waste of ammo and time."

"Sure, but if we ignore them and they follow us all the way to the refinery, we might end up having to deal with them behind us and the Brotherhood in front." Shay shrugged. "There's only the two of us. Sure, we're badasses, but it helps not to hand the enemy an advantage."

"Sounds like the Sun Tzu shit the guys are always spouting." James frowned. "Shit, probably should take care of them sooner; less chance of the car getting damaged. Stupid fucking weak-ass insurance."

She laughed. "Okay. Why not just pull off the road so we can get this shit taken care of?"

He tugged the wheel to the right. The vehicle shook as it left the smooth highway and entered the snow-covered field running alongside it. A dense stand of aspens bounded the field, but James stopped well before the tree line.

James reached under his jacket. "Might as well get this shit over with. He's gonna annoy the fuck out of me until we get to the refinery, though."

"Hey, it's a small price to pay for what he gives you." Shay nodded and pulled out her 9mm.

"You don't have to listen to him in your head." James removed the spacer beneath his amulet and hissed as pain shot from the point of contact with his chest, each tendril of the amulet spreading out underneath his skin, joining with his flesh and hardening it.

*Initiation*, Whispy sent.

James took several deep breaths as the amulet finished bonding to him.

The SUVs slowed as they closed on the Jeep, which might be evidence of possible trouble or maybe people concerned that James and Shay were having trouble. They would find out soon enough.

*Engage and kill all enemies*, the amulet ordered. *Adapt and grow stronger. Achieve primary directive.*

*Tell me what your primary directive is and maybe I can help get you there quicker.*

*Achieve primary directive by engaging and killing new enemies. Achieve maximum adaptation.*

*That's how, not what.*

*Achieve primary directive by engaging and killing new enemies.*

James grunted. "Fucking useless."

"What?" Shay frowned.

"Whispy Doom's stonewalling when I ask him questions. Not sure if he doesn't know or if he's just fucking with me." James shook his head. "It doesn't matter. I'll find out eventually." He threw open the door and stepped out. "Let's handle this shit for now."

Shay stepped out on the opposite side and flipped her hood over her head. "It's not so cold. Not like Antarctica."

James shrugged. With Whispy bonded, he barely noticed the temperature. He stood there, his arms at his sides, waiting for the SUVs to finish their approach. All three closed to within ten yards and pulled off the road in a line.

He walked away from the Jeep, leaving large footprints in the accumulated snow.

*Let's do this shit.*

Shay reached into her pocket to pull out a ring and murmured an incantation. A faint golden glow surrounded her and reflected off the bright white snow on the ground.

The doors to the SUVs all flew open at the same time, and twelve men in white and gray camouflage leapt out of the vehicles. A half-dozen pointed stun rifles, the others regular assault rifles. The men wore belts with clipped grenades, frag and stun, along with holstered sidearms.

"Mercenaries," James muttered. "This shit is annoying."

*Lack of additional useful adaptation anticipated. Kill enemies rapidly and proceed to current primary mission objective.*

James snorted. Whispy had gotten steadily mouthier and wordier in recent months, but the amulet had never chastised him for not being fast to arrive at a job.

*Don't worry, this won't take long. I think I liked you better when you just whispered and I couldn't understand you. Now you're just annoying.*

*Kill enemies.*

*Was gonna do that anyway.*

Shay kept her 9mm pointed at the ground. James didn't draw his weapon. If they were going to fight, he was going to go either Yeti or Wendigo on them.

James shook his head and sighed. "I don't know who the fuck you are, but you're obviously not the Brotherhood of Silence if you're showing up with stun rifles. Gonna tell you right now that shit doesn't work on me, and if you're not the Brotherhood, I've got no reason to kill you. Walk the fuck away while you still can. The only reason I haven't killed you already is that I have no fucking idea who you are."

One of the men took a step forward, his boots sinking into the snow. "You should have never come to Canada, Brownstone."

James snorted. "You sound American."

"So what if I am?"

"Don't care that much. Just means the Canadian rep for being friendly lasts a little longer, not counting that Customs asshole." James shrugged. "It also means me being in Canada is none of your fucking business."

The mercenary clucked his tongue. "We've been paid to make it our business."

Shay continued to watch, stone-faced.

The mercenary chuckled, along with several of the others. "If you put your weapons down, turn around right now, and drop to your knees, we'll put cuffs on and you won't die right here in some piss-ant nowhere field in the middle of Alberta. Don't worry, Brownstone, special cuffs, they'll work even on you. Even if you're tempted to escape, it won't matter."

James grunted. "And who the fuck are you that I should take that offer instead of snapping your neck and beating your buddies to death with your body?"

"The people who are going to fucking kill you otherwise, tough guy." The man grinned. "I get paid either way, but I figure I can probably squeeze out a bonus if I take you alive. If you insist on dying, though, we can make that happen."

A gust of wind coated them all with snow.

Shay snorted. "Are you really that stupid?"

"Who the fuck are you, bitch?" The mercenary glared at her.

James shook his head. "You really *are* a dumb asshole, aren't you?"

Shay brushed snow out of her face. "You guys are lucky. We're trying to show fucking restraint here, but you're just begging us to kill you." She pointed at the sky. "We've got somewhere to go, and the weather's shitty. It's been a really annoying trip, and we've only been here for a day. Just get back in your SUVs and drive the fuck away before you die."

The man snorted. "Fuck this shit. Stun 'em."

The stun rifles buzzed, the blue bolts zipping across the snow-covered field toward Shay and James. Four bolts slammed into James.

He grunted and stumbled back, his muscles twitching.

*Near maximum adaptation against existing attack achieved. Kill targets and proceed to current primary mission objective.*

Two bolts hit Shay. The golden field around her brightened, and she didn't flinch.

She whipped up her 9mm and took three quick shots. The heads of three men exploded, splattering blood all over the white snow.

James didn't grab his gun. He charged with a growl. The remaining nine men snapped their rifles toward him and opened fire, a cloud of blue bolts and bullets ripping into his coat. The attacks stung but didn't pierce his skin.

It only took him seconds to reach the closest man. He yanked the rifle out of his hand and cracked the weapon across the mercenary's head, producing an audible crunch. When he let go, the weapon was embedded in the man's skull.

The remaining men intensified their attacks, switching the assault rifles to full auto. Their rifles spat a stream of bullets toward James. They bounced off, crushed and ineffective. The stun rifle holders dropped the non-lethal weapons to the ground and pulled out sidearms. They opened fire and added to the bullet storm, but accomplished nothing except the further shredding of James' ugly gray parka.

*Fuck. I should have brought more than the one parka. This shit means I'll have to stay bonded to Whispy.*

Whispy radiated irritation. *Kill enemies. Near maximum adaptation against existing attack achieved. Adaptational usefulness limited.*

*Not having fun? I thought you loved it when I killed people.*

*Adaptational usefulness limited. Further adaptation necessary to achieve primary directive.*

*You used to be cooler when you didn't try to boss me around.*

James grinned. He yanked out a throwing knife and launched it into the head of another man. A second thrown knife killed the man beside him.

The mercenaries backed up, more anger than fear on their faces. Two more men screamed as Shay put rounds into them.

The enemy sprinted back and took cover behind one of the SUVs.

Shay laughed. "You stupid dumbasses should have waited and taken us on in a building, or even at the refinery. Now you've got nowhere to hide. Did you assholes even do any research? Did you think a few rifles were going to take down James Brownstone? Fuck, you can't even take *me* down with that shit anymore."

Two frag grenades arced through the air toward Shay. "Better."

She jumped backward as the grenades exploded, her golden aura glowing even brighter. The force knocked her to the ground.

James leapt onto the hood of the SUV and yanked out his .45. The men in the front opened fire again and backed away slowly. Their bullets bounced off the bounty hunter and landed in the thin layer of snow on the hood.

He took careful aim at a man's head and pulled the trigger, and a follow-up shot finished off another mercenary.

One of the two remaining men charged Brownstone, a frag grenade in hand. "Fuck you, Brownstone. If I'm going down, you're going down with me, you sonofabitch."

James ignored the man to put three rounds into the chest of the other mercenary.

The charging man's eyes gleamed with malice as he crashed into James. The grenade exploded, and the blast shredded what remained of James' coat and shirt, revealing the hardened skin underneath and leaving a few lacerations. Full armor might have stopped it completely, but he wasn't pissed enough to even bother asking for it.

*Shit, that actually hurt a little. Will that regenerate?*

*Regeneration in progress. Avoid additional damage during regeneration period.*

James wiped the mercenary's blood off his face and turned around. Shay was already up, an annoyed look on her face.

She pointed at him. "You're covered in that guy's blood and guts. You do kind of have a killer Yeti-slash-Wendigo thing going on after all."

*Proceed to current primary mission objective,* Whispy demanded. *Regeneration will continue.*

*Keep your pants on.*

*Illogical request of enhancement symbiont.*

*Enhancement symbiont? That's what you call yourself? And it was a joke.*

*Refrain from non-tactical requests for maximum tactical efficiency.*

James chuckled and shook his head. *Fuck you. You've been riding my mind for years, and now you're pissed because I'm actually thinking at you? You don't call the shots.*

*Link error acknowledged.*

*What the fuck does that mean?*

*Proceed to current primary mission objective. Find new enemies. Kill new enemies. Achieve maximum adaptation.*

James didn't have time to argue with the petulant amulet, although he had a feeling Whispy had let something important slip. The amulet liked to give him orders and always seemed frustrated when the bounty hunter didn't do exactly what he was told.

*That wasn't how this was supposed to work, was it, Whispy Doom?*

*Proceed to current primary mission objective. Find new enemies. Kill new enemies.*

James grunted and marched through the snow to Shay. "You okay?"

She nodded. "Wasted more of the charge on my ring than I would have wanted, but I didn't get hurt. You?"

"A few scratches, but it'll heal." He nodded over his shoulder. "Clueless." He gestured to his shredded shirt and pants. "Glad I brought some extra clothes."

Shay pulled her ring off and her glow faded. She walked over to the nearest body, her boots crunching in the snow, and searched through the corpse's pocket until she found a phone.

She held it up. "Peyton or Heather can check this shit out later and figure out who these fools were."

James nodded slowly, wondering if he should tell Shay what he'd just figured out about the amulet, but decided against it. Despite the hassle at the airport and the delay, kicking a little ass had perked him up.

*Shay is right. Sometimes you* do *just need to get it out of your system. We can worry about mouthy control-freak amulet briefings later.*

The snow swirled around them, the harsh wind heaping the snow into drifts.

James headed toward the Jeep. "Let's get going before the storm gets worse. We're closer to the refinery than a city now anyway."

*Time to go for that primary mission objective.*

# CHAPTER THIRTEEN

Trey strolled into the seedy bar. Thick smoke choked the air, along with a heady mixture of BO and fetid breath.

*Damn. Haven't any of these guys ever heard of a shower or brushing their teeth?*

The bounty hunter wrinkled his nose, taking pride in the fact that even when he had been a criminal, he hadn't let himself go like the men filling the room.

He didn't spot a single woman in the place, not even a waitress; just dangerous men, many with scars, and a few with bandanas or tattoos marking them as members of local gangs. He shook his head.

*Damn. Makes the Black Sun seem like the classiest joint in the country. Have to tell Tyler that the next time I see him.*

Trey laughed at the thought. He'd been a gangbanger not all that long ago, but now the lifestyle seemed like a pathetic dead end. It was hard to believe he'd ever thought he could focus so much on short-term violence. Even if his current lifestyle wasn't exactly full of pacifism, James, Staff

Sergeant Royce, and others offered a vision for the future besides controlling some small slice of turf and dying young.

*Have I really changed or have I just joined a tougher gang with a tougher gang leader? Don't matter much. Suppose what I'm about to do when I find this sonofabitch ain't that different from what I was doing before, but respect is respect.*

Trey had visited more than a few dives and spent the day touring the darker parts of Las Vegas in pursuit of the thief. A few answers pointed him toward his current unpleasant environment.

Deafening rock music blasted from the speakers as Trey maneuvered through the room toward a table in the back. A wrinkled old man wearing an ill-fitting suit and sporting a bad bronze spray tan sat there. The man took a long drag from his cigarette as the bounty hunter closed on him.

"Hey," Trey began, "You Anthony? 'Cause you look like him."

The man blew the smoke in Trey's face. "Maybe. Who the fuck are you, and why should I care?"

*Won't do me no good to knock his ass out even if he is a little bitch.*

Trey coughed and waved the smoke out of his face. "Someone's looking for information, and I checked around and heard you might be able to help me with said information."

"And how can I help you?"

"I heard you're a man who likes to pay for shit people find," Trey replied.

"Lots of people help lots of other people. And lots of people hear lots of things." Anthony stubbed his cigarette out in a glass ashtray. "And, yeah, maybe I pay for a few things here and there when people happen to find them and bring them to me." He smirked. "You think I don't know who you are, Trey Garfield? You and your Brownstone buddies are walking around swinging your dicks like you own the town. Half of fucking Vegas knows who you are."

"That's the damned point." Trey shrugged. "And good that you know already. That makes this shit simple. I ain't got no beef with you, but I *do* have a beef with the fucker who broke into Jessie Rae's."

Anthony picked up a half-empty glass of beer and took a sip, his brow furrowed in confusion "The barbeque place?"

"Yeah. The barbeque place."

Anthony frowned. "What's any of this shit have to do with me?"

"Along with other shit, some trophies and plaques got stolen. Awards for winning competitions." Trey chuckled and shook his head. "The dumbass motherfucker who did this probably thought they were gold. He goes to a pawn shop or something, the people gonna spot his stolen shit all the way from Oriceran. But he goes to someone with a little more discretion or who gives less of a fuck, and maybe he can make a little money. I'm sure that person, that fence, knows exactly who this fucker is."

The fence narrowed his eyes. "You think I ran into the guy? You think he tried to sell me the shit from Jessie Rae's? I'm big-time. I don't need no trophies from a barbeque place."

Trey's face twitched. Breaking Anthony's nose wouldn't

get him the information he needed, and he knew the bastard had it. This was no fishing expedition, but it'd help if he let the fence believe it was.

"I think you're a man who can take care of shit, and so why wouldn't the thief show up and chat with you?" Trey shrugged. "Look, I'm not asking for anything other than confirmation. I ain't the 5-0. You don't have to testify or shit like that. I just need a name, and I'm willing to pay for it, probably a lot more than you can make selling whatever the asshole gave you."

Anthony shrugged. "If I send bounty hunters after people who sell to me, that's gonna be bad for future business. You need to see this from my perspective."

*Time for a little "What would the big man do?"*

Trey pulled a chair back and sat. He reached into his pockets and retrieved his gloves. After sliding them on, he offered a thin smile to Anthony.

The fence snorted. "What? Am I supposed to be scared because you put on some cheap-ass gloves?"

Trey raised his hand and shook a finger at Anthony. "My girlfriend gave these to me, and they ain't cheap-ass, but I'm gonna let that shit pass and ask you another question. Do you really want to piss me off, Anthony?" His smile disappeared. "Lots of other shit I can let slide, but not fucking with Jessie Rae's. This ain't about you giving people up to bounty hunters; this is about some fucker who shouldn't have messed with a place protected by the Brownstone Agency. He disrespected Jessie Rae's. He disrespected the Brownstone Agency, and shit, he disrespected James Brownstone." He laughed. "You're lucky I'm here and not the big man. *He* might have thrown your ass through a wall already for not giving up the thief right away."

"You think threats are gonna work on me, bounty hunter? You think you're the first fucker to ever walk in and say shit like that?" Anthony shrugged. "Please."

"Don't know about other assholes. Only know about me. Though I've been asking myself lately: how fun is it to throw shitbags through walls? Big man's done it a lot. Has to be at least a little bit fun, don't you think?" Trey offered the fence a feral grin. "But we don't have to be uncivilized like that. We can handle this like businessmen.

Anthony narrowed his eyes. "Businessmen?"

Trey nodded and reached into his pocket to pull out his wallet. He fished out several large bills and tossed them on the table. "Give me a fucking name, and I walk out of this nasty-ass place and leave you alone. Don't give me a name, and we might have trouble that ends with me throwing you through a wall."

Anthony crossed his arms. "You don't look so tough."

The bounty hunter held up a gloved hand. "By the way, that girlfriend who gave these gloves to me? She's a witch, motherfucker."

The other man stared at Trey's hand. "You're saying they're magic?"

"I'm saying my fingers are twitching to test the strength of the walls in this place." Trey shook his head and sighed. "But you see, my nana, she would be pretty fucking pissed at me if I beat down some old man, even if he's a piece of shit who should probably be rotting in a cell somewhere, so I'd really, *really* prefer not to have to do that."

Anthony swallowed.

Trey slid the money toward Anthony. "It's not like you bought the shit, did you? Wait." He laughed. "Not the plaques. No money in it. Too traceable. But you brought the fucking tv, didn't you? Mister Big Time buying tvs."

The fence's face twitched. "Fuck you, Garfield."

"Here, this is how nice I am. I don't even give a shit about the tv. Insurance will cover that." Trey shook his head. "But those trophies and plaques—I need to get those back, and the thief, well, he needs to understand there are certain places you don't touch because you'll draw the wrong kind of attention." He leaned forward and locked eyes with Anthony. "Last chance, motherfucker, before I start practicing what my boss has been doing for years."

"Demetrius," Anthony snapped. "I don't know his last name. I know he lives in Huntridge because he mentioned it. I can describe him, but I don't have a picture or anything."

Trey held up a hand. "Don't need that. I already have a picture. Demetrius, you see, is a dumb motherfucker in addition to being a thief." He patted the money. "Enjoy the payday, Anthony. If Demetrius comes sniffing around again, you tell him Trey Garfield's coming for him."

Anthony blinked. "You *want* him to know you're coming?"

Trey grinned. "Yeah. I want that motherfucker to sweat so much he runs to the police to turn his ass in."

The fence shook his head. "He's not gonna do that. You know he's not a normal thief. I saw it. He's got himself this magic knife. You might be biting off more than you can chew, Garfield."

Trey stood and adjusted his tie. "Just more fun for me

then, and besides, the big man will be coming to the show."

"The big man...you mean Brownstone?" Anthony paled.

"Yeah. Like I said, Demetrius is a dumb motherfucker."

---

The falling snow cut visibility to a few yards, and the howling wind sounded like an angry ghost waiting for Shay and James to become its victims. The Jeep continued chugging along what remained of the dirt road they were following to the refinery. They hadn't run into any other mercenaries, or anything more interesting than snow-covered trees.

James glanced down at the GPS. "We're almost there. I can't see shit, but we're almost there."

Heather sighed. She and Peyton had been monitoring the situation and staying in touch through the speakerphone.

"What's wrong?" James asked.

"The storm's not going to clear for hours," Heather explained. "The drones wouldn't survive thirty seconds in the air. We're not going to be able to do much to back you up."

"She's right, you know," Peyton added. "Maybe you should hold your position for a few hours."

James grunted. "This isn't the kind of job we need babysitters on, and I'm not sitting around in a Jeep not doing shit for several hours because of a little snow. I don't like the cold, but I'm not afraid of it. If a Yeti shows up, I'll kick his ass."

"Aren't Yetis more of a Himalayan thing?" Peyton asked.

"Point is, just some fucking snow."

"Not like it's flying," Shay murmured under her breath.

James shot her a dirty look, and she shrugged.

"But you know someone's watching you," Heather complained. "After what happened with the mercenaries, I doubt we can just write it off as Canadian intelligence. More mercenaries will probably show up. You can't depend on them trying to take you alive. What if they surprise you and shoot off a missile or rocket while you're still driving?"

James let up on the gas slightly. "Don't know. Don't give a fuck at this point. Got plenty of ammo left for them. If they *do* get the drop on us, they better finish us off with the first fucking attack or they're all dead."

Peyton groaned. "Shay, can't you talk to him?"

She snickered. "I know what you two are saying, but it cuts both ways. If we can't see shit, then the Brotherhood can't see shit. Neither can any mercenary assholes who want a piece of James, rocket launchers or not. By the time the storm clears, we'll have cleared out the Brotherhood, so if a few more mercenaries show up, it'll be no big deal."

"Exactly," James rumbled. "This isn't some fancy shit where we need you to hack doors and watch for enemy drones. This is just us killing twisted fuckers. No evacuation. No worries about them running like little fucking roaches through portals. We show up. They surrender, or they die. Simple. Just the way I like it."

Despite James' mention of killing, Whispy remained silent. The amulet had been quiet since the encounter with the mercenaries, although something approaching frustration and irritation leaked from it.

*Are you fucking pouting?*

The amulet didn't respond.

*Whatever. Do what the fuck you need to do when the time comes. I like it better when you keep your fucking thoughts to yourself.*

The Jeep shook for a moment, and loud static filled the phone line.

"Shit," James muttered, glancing down at his phone. "We lost signal."

Shay frowned. "Off a high-powered satellite phone? Even with this storm, it should still be getting a signal."

James shrugged. "Technology isn't perfect."

"Maybe you have a shitty phone." Shay pulled out her phone and dialed. After a few seconds, her frown deepened. "I don't think this is just a satellite hiccup. I think something's blocking the signal, which is damned suspicious considering we don't have any mountains or major hills around." She pointed to the console screen.

**GPS SIGNAL LOST. ATTEMPTING RECONNECTION...**

The Jeep slowed more as James let up on the gas, his eyes narrowed. The headlights illuminated a partially collapsed metal fence through the raging snow. The outlines of small buildings showed in front of the massive cylindrical storage tanks, their white color making them disappear in the blizzard. A central building filled with mechanical spires and a latticework of metal formed the center of the facility.

"We're here." James stopped the Jeep. "The Brotherhood must have some spell set up."

"That might also mean they know we're here." Shay

looked at James. "And they'll be prepared."

"They can prepare all they want. They won't be prepared for me."

*Locate and kill all enemies,* Whispy sent. *Adaptation potential moderate. Achieve primary directive.*

*Oh, you wake up for the good shit?*

James grinned and threw open the door. The muffled cry of the wind grew deafening. Clouds of snow flowed over the land, doing their best to bury everything in their path.

Shay let out a low chuckle. "Fuck it. Next time, we're going to a his-and-hers ass-kicking in the Caribbean."

James raised an eyebrow. "I thought you'd been to Antarctica."

"I have, and it was fucking cold there, too." Shay shrugged. "What can I say? When you're right, you're right."

James grunted. "I should record that shit. Might not ever hear it again."

"Probably." Shay reached into the back seat to grab her AK and a few more grenades for her belt, along with her sword belt holding her Masamune *tachi.* Being geared up, complete with a sword, made sitting in the Jeep uncomfortable, but they'd be leaving soon enough.

James had replaced his shirt and pants earlier, but the front of his parka was still a bullet-riddled mess. Whispy was keeping the cold from being all that noticeable. James wondered if he could run around naked with the damned thing on and barely feel the temperature.

Shay handed James a headlamp before slipping on her own and putting her AR goggles in her pocket. Even though it was still daylight, they had no idea if any of the buildings would have decent light, and they wanted their hands free for weapons. From the looks of things, he doubted they'd restored electricity to the place, and it'd been abandoned for decades.

"They are right, you know." Shay shrugged. "We could sit and wait for the storm to die down."

James shook his head. "Nah. It'll be easier to pick the Brotherhood off one by one this way." He stepped out of the Jeep and peered into swirling snow. "And if they did know we're here, they could have thrown a spell or some shit at us, but nothing. From what the Professor sent us in the briefing files, most of the Brotherhood relies on magically-enhanced hand-to-hand anyway." He grunted. "Their mistake, if they're going to be fighting me."

Shay took a deep breath, opened her door, and stepped out. She shook out her white-gloved hands. "Let's find some asshole to kill. It'll warm me up. They might want to punch someone with a fire fist or whatever, but I'm just going to shoot them. It's what field archaeologists do. Just ask Indiana Jones."

*You good with keeping me warm?* James thought.

*Temperature regulation will require minor realignment of general defenses, with minor overall efficiency reduction.*

*Fine. Not like these fuckers are gonna require advanced mode.*

*Insufficient power for advanced transformation.*

James grunted. *I know.*

He slammed his door shut, the noise swallowed by the wind, and waded through the already-deep snow. Shay stomped toward him.

"Want to retire up here?" she asked. "I'm sure there's great skiing, or you can take up hockey."

"I don't fall down mountains on purpose." James continued toward the fence. "And I don't play games."

"Don't I know it."

A dark mound right past an opening in the fence caught James' attention. He pulled out his .45.

Shay raised her AK. They both crept forward and kept their weapons trained at the dark mound in the snow.

*Kill enemy,* Whispy demanded.

The pair closed on the mound and realized it was a man partially buried by snow, most of his face obscured under layers of white precipitation. They aimed their weapons and waited for the man to spring his attack, but after thirty seconds he hadn't so much as twitched.

*Kill enemy.*

*Yeah, this guy's real threatening. I think someone already did that.*

James holstered his pistol. "Cover me."

Shay nodded and kept her rifle trained at the man.

The bounty hunter stomped through the snow and knelt. He brushed some of the white off the man and realized they weren't looking at a Brotherhood assassin lying in wait or stunned, but a corpse.

Dusting off the snow revealed hints of a layer of splattered blood on the snow around the man. His left arm was missing, a frozen and torn stump left in its place. A wide-eyed expression of terror was fixed on the man's face. His face was covered with deep scars carved to form intricate arcane glyphs, which proved he was a member of the Brotherhood. Deep tears marred his shirt, along with huge ragged parallel gouges in his flesh.

"What the fuck?" Shay muttered. "That looks like claw marks."

"Yeah." James grunted. "Get up close and personal with a bear?"

Shay shook her head. "A bear that ripped his arm clean off and then just took off?" She surveyed the area. "Too much fucking snow. No tracks." She pointed with the rifle behind James. "Even our tracks are getting filled in quickly."

"If it wasn't a bear, then what was it?" James stood and shrugged.

Shay sighed. "We're raiding a cult led by a dark wizard with a powerful artifact. I'm guessing he tried to summon something that got out of hand, and it's angry and hungry."

*Find and kill the new enemy,* Whispy ordered. *Adaptational potential high. Achieve primary directive.*

*How did I know you'd be happy when we found a torn-apart body?*

James frowned. "Maybe, or maybe not."

"What do *you* think, then?" Shay peered into the snowy haze. "Just a wild animal? I might not be Wilderness Jane, but I've hit the countryside a lot more than you have. I know when I'm not looking at an animal attack."

He shook his head. "Just because the Professor knew about the Brotherhood being here doesn't mean he was the only one. I think another bounty hunter showed up. They were probably behind getting Customs to fuck with me, and the mercenaries. They were trying to slow me down."

"A bounty hunter who rips off arms and claws people?"

Shay eyed James.

"I've done worse. Maybe he's collecting arms instead of heads for his bounty credit." He shrugged. "Could be a wizard who summoned shit to help him, or a shifter." He gritted his teeth. "Flew all the way up to Alberta in the damned snow, and some other fucker's gonna get all my bounty money."

Shay shrugged. "Well, it's the Canadian government. It's not like they require heads. Tissue samples and pictures should be enough."

James shook his head. "Not if the other guy finishes them all off first."

"What do you want to do? I know what I'd do if I were on a tomb raid." Shay raised an eyebrow in question.

James kicked some snow over the dead cultist. "Not gonna kill a bounty hunter for getting somewhere before me. That's not how I work."

Shay blew out a breath. "Fine, but he's a bounty hunter, not a tomb raider, which means we can play this a little differently."

"Meaning what? You want to kill him instead of me?"

She shook her head. "Meaning we can at least still score the artifact. If there *is* another bounty hunter, he might not know about the urn, but my money's still on bad summoning."

Gusts of wind blasted the top of a nearby snowdrift over the body. Only its wide eyes remained uncovered.

James nodded. "Fine. We'll just continue to look for people. If we kill some of them, we can still at least get some credit, and this trip won't be a total waste of time."

He shook his head. *My fucking luck.*

# CHAPTER FOURTEEN

Peyton frowned as he entered another series of commands to reroute his transmission pathway through a different satellite. A few seconds passed, and the same error messages popped up.

"Damn it," he shouted.

His cat yowled and hopped off his computer desk, rushing out of the back office of Warehouse Two.

"It's okay," Heather responded through his headset. "We'll figure something out."

Peyton glanced at the window containing Heather's webcam image. Judging by her face, she didn't look that worried, but he still wasn't convinced everything was fine.

"Maybe, but I don't know why we've lost comm." Peyton popped up another satellite display. "Do you? From what I can tell, EM interference isn't even that severe. I've been able to reestablish a connection with Shay in way worse conditions than this."

"Come on, Peyton, we both know what happened. Our bosses are going after a magical cult." Heather sighed. "The cult must have put up some sort of spell, and unless you've hidden some magical ability that you haven't told anyone about, there's not much we can do about it."

"Stupid magic," he muttered. "It's messing with my awesomeness." He harrumphed.

"Not our first time dealing with this kind of thing." The background clack of Heather typing came over the comm. "And as much as it annoys me, they're right. If James and Shay can take on the Council, they can take on the Brotherhood. Even if the storm clears up, the drones are still in the damned Jeep, so there's nothing we can do until they contact us again."

Peyton rubbed his chin and snapped, "We can hack a drone or two in Calgary and fly it over. Maybe a military one."

"Just what we need, the Canadian military following us." Heather laughed. "Even if we did that, whatever's happening will be over by the time the storm clears enough for us to get a drone there. You really think James and Shay are suddenly going to decide to sit and wait because of a little weather?"

Peyton snapped his fingers. "You know what we need?"

"A magic wand that clears up snow?"

"Some sort of sentry bot." Peyton nodded. "They can pack it along, and then we can join the action even if the weather is bad."

Heather snorted. "We'd still have lost the link."

"You're right." Peyton rubbed the back of his neck. "But what do we do in the mean—"

"Quiet." Heather hunched over her keyboard and typed furiously, her face pinched in concentration.

"What the hell, Heather? I know the idea wasn't that practical, but no reason to talk to me like that."

"Let me concentrate." Heather narrowed her eyes, and her brow furrowed. Her fingers continued to dance over the keyboard. After a few seconds, she shook her head. "Check your system. I think someone just tried to trace me off the satellite I was using to try to reconnect to James' phone. Weird signature. Something feels off about it."

"What the hell?" Peyton frowned and executed a few quick defensive scripts, glancing at a side monitor to check on the results. "Shit. There was definitely something there, but it's gone now. You still under attack?"

"Maybe." Heather hissed. "Trying to trace it back to the source. Can't believe these assholes came at me directly. Ballsy."

Peyton nodded and initiated his own trace. No enemy could come at him and just run away. His pride was at stake. Both hackers worked their fingers and their programs to try to identify whoever had struck at them in cyberspace.

After several minutes, Peyton sat back and ran his fingers through his hair. "Shit. Whoever it was, they're gone. Clean trail. I keep dead-ending at proxies. Any luck?"

Heather shook her head. "No. Similar signature to whoever was hunting James before, though. It's definitely a repeat offender."

"Don't ever tell Shay I said this, but whoever is doing this is good." Peyton took a deep breath. "Like scary good. Maybe even better than us."

Heather shook her head. "Better than us individually, not better than us together."

Peyton blinked a few times and nodded. "Let's hope so."

---

Aiyn glared at her display. It was absurd that despite all the advanced technology she had available to her, normal humans could defend against her electronic warfare.

"If you people used something more advanced than children's toys, it wouldn't be the same."

That wasn't the only issue. She couldn't reestablish a link to the units she'd sent into the refinery, even if she had been able to harden them against the electrical suppression field the cult had apparently thrown up. She wasn't sure if it was in response to Brownstone or her forces, but it didn't matter. In either event, she'd underestimated the flexibility of the Brotherhood's magic.

"More surprises in the snow. No matter. If it ends with Brownstone dead, I don't care."

---

James and Shay trekked away from the body toward a long, narrow, windowless building near the fence line. A single large pair of metal doors stood in the middle, both closed. There was no sign of bodies or other bounty hunters.

The harsh wind continued to push the snow into drifts on the ground and the roofs of the complex. The central building was connected to several smaller buildings by covered metal tunnels, and the storage tanks via pipes.

James closed on the doors. A simple latch secured them. He narrowed his eyes and gestured to a faint handprint.

Given the wind and snow, someone had exited or entered the building recently.

Shay nodded and raised her gun.

With a quick movement, James unlatched the door and slid the two metal doors apart. The beam of his headlight penetrated the dark, unlit interior. He paused and frowned at a blood smear running across the back wall. A dead cultist lay against the wall, his head hanging forward and a large chunk of his shoulder missing, along with half an arm and a leg.

Whispy beamed pure joy at the sight.

*You're such a twisted fuck.*

James turned his head, his light illuminating another body. A second later he realized it was a standing cultist, his face covered with blood.

The cultist charged James, a crazed look in his eyes and his fists glowing red. His magically powered fist slammed into the bounty hunter. James grunted as pain spiked from his chest, followed by a burning sensation.

*Yes. New adaptation achieved. Kill enemy.*

James threw up an arm to block the next hit. Another jolt of burning pain shot from his arm, but its intensity was much lower than the first. He threw a wide hook, his fist landing on the side of his opponent's head. The man spun several times before crashing to the hard metal floor.

Rifle shots echoed behind James, and he pivoted. Two cultists lay on the floor, bullet holes in the centers of their heads.

Shay frowned at the bodies. "What the hell?"

James grunted and stumbled, the burning sensation strengthening and spreading through the rest of his body.

*I thought you adapted to this shit, Whispy.*

*Full adaptation not available during previous attacks. Systemic effect will be blocked in future attacks. Systematic regeneration insufficient for current damage.*

*Fucking wonderful. I'm glad it'll help going forward when I'm fucking on fire now.*

Burning agony shot through James' body, and he fell to his knees.

Shay slung her rifle over her shoulder and rushed to his side. "What's wrong?"

"Some sort of magical poison," James growled through gritted teeth. He yanked a healing potion from a belt pouch and downed the contents.

The seconds stretched as an inferno built in every part of his body. His vision wavered. The inferno faded to a mere fire before all the pain disappeared entirely.

James took a deep breath and stood, shaking out his arms. "It shouldn't be a problem next time, but you better use your ring. If one of these guys hits you once, it'll fuck you up."

Shay nodded and pulled out her ring. She murmured an incantation, and a golden aura surrounded her.

She gestured to the dead body along the wall. "I don't get it. Someone slipped in here and ripped that guy to shreds but left everyone else alive?"

James walked over to the men Shay had shot, moving his head a little to light different parts of their bodies. He frowned and gestured. "Look at the bodies. I didn't notice in the fight, but one of these guys is missing a hand, another has been clawed in the back." He knelt and turned one of the corpse's heads. He gestured to several tears in the side of his neck. "More claws. Your bullets finished them off, but they probably wouldn't have made it."

They headed over to the man who'd struck James. The cultist groaned and rolled onto his back.

Shay yanked her AK down and pointed at the man. James grunted and pulled his .45 out of its holster.

*Kill enemy,* Whispy demanded.

James ignored his amulet and focused on the man. The bloody and battered side of his face was evidence of the bounty hunter's blow, but now that the cultist wasn't moving, James noticed the shredded fabric in his baggy pants and the deep slashes in his leg. Some of the wounds extended to the bone.

"Huh," Shay murmured. "Must have some sort of pain-suppressing spell on them, given the way they were moving even with those wounds."

The cultist's eyes flicked open. "You think you've won anything?" he rasped.

James shrugged. "Bunch of dead assholes and I'm still alive. You got a couple of nice hits on me, but I'm not burning up on the inside or whatever was supposed to happen. So, yeah, I won."

The cultist's face twisted in anger, and he coughed up blood. "It...doesn't matter."

"Doesn't matter?" James glanced at Shay before looking back down at the man. "And why is that? I already told you that your little magical attack failed."

"Because the Wendigo will get you too. You...won't... leave...here...alive." The cultist's head slumped to the side, and he stopped breathing.

Shay clucked her tongue. "That answers that. I wasn't sure about us having shit luck before, but that seals it."

James snorted. "You believe that bullshit?"

"About the Wendigo?" Shay nodded. "Why wouldn't I?"

"He's just trying to get in our heads." James snorted. "Maybe the fuckers are killing themselves. Some sort of power struggle."

Shay pointed at the slashes. "Not seeing claws on any of these guys. The guy who hit you had glowing poison hands, not claws." She shook her head. "And if it was something they summoned, like the kind of shit we saw the Council use, I don't think he would have called it a Wendigo."

*All local enemies killed,* Whispy sent. *Find new enemies. Kill enemies. Maximize adaptation to achieve primary directive.*

*Fuck you. We'll take our time.*

James frowned, trying his best to ignore the amulet. "So you're telling me some fucking cannibal spirit is running around slicing up and eating cultists?"

Shay stared at him. "Why the hell not? I've done raids on haunted fucking houses and fought weirder shit, like those frog guys in Russia or the damned bunyip in Australia." She shook her head. "That's the problem with all the magic returning to the world. A lot of those legendary creatures aren't just legends anymore." She laughed. "Hell, think of the shit we've both seen at the School of Necessary Magic!"

"You mean like that fucking ferret with the top hat?" James glared around the building as if the creature would appear. "He thinks he's so damned fancy."

"I was thinking more about unicorns and Kirin." Shay

shrugged. "But, sure, ferrets with top hats are totally on the same level as cannibal spirits ripping people's arms off and eating them."

James grunted. "Yeah."

Shay smirked.

*What's she smiling about?*

James searched the dark corners of the room to make sure there were no more hidden cultists. "Doubt it's another bounty hunter, even a shifter. This shit is too messed up."

"Yeah, because it's a Wendigo." Shay rolled her eyes. "Don't know why it's so hard to accept. You've fought necromancers, giant weird Oriceran monsters, and whatever the hell He Who Hunts was, but you draw the line at Wendigos?"

"Got to draw the line somewhere." James shrugged. "Doesn't matter. All we have to do is find this thing and fucking waste it. If it's just some messed-up monster, Wendigo or whatever, then I don't give a fuck about poaching the bounties from him, since he's doing the same to me. He can fuck off and go eat a moose somewhere."

Shay ejected her magazine and stuck it in a pouch. She pulled out a magazine of anti-magic bullets and slapped it into her rifle. "Maybe the Wendigo was attracted to this area because of all the blood sacrifice. So they did summon it, just not the way they thought. Or, shit, for all we know, maybe the Wendigo was the reason they abandoned this refinery to begin with. Not like governments were all that honest back in the day, and this place dates from before the full return of magic."

"I don't give a shit why," James replied. "If it's just

running around biting people and clawing them, I won't even need advanced mode. It'll barely be able to scratch me."

*Insufficient power for advanced transformation,* Whispy complained. *Find new enemy. Kill new enemy. Adaptation potential moderate.*

*Don't you worry,* James thought back. *Fucker's making something simple complicated. I'd take him out for that alone.*

Shay headed toward the door. "Well, if it *is* a Wendigo, we better not give it a chance to eat anyone whole if we want to get credit."

James kicked at the ground. "Fucking Wendigos. I'll show them who the real monster is."

# CHAPTER FIFTEEN

James wouldn't have thought it possible, but more snow choked the air. The harsh wind kept blasting flakes into his face, and even if their cold touch didn't bother him much, the lack of visibility was annoying him more than he had expected.

*This is why I've stayed in LA. Fuck snow. Fuck blizzards.*

"We can't do anything in this weather, James," Shay shouted, the only way she could be heard over the wind. "Can you see anything? Because I can't."

He shook his head. "A building in front of us, but nothing else. No horizon, no nothing."

Shay reached into her pocket and pulled out her AR goggles. She slid them over her eyes and tapped at the side with a frown. "Command, visual mode two," she shouted. After a few seconds, her frown deepened. "Fucking perfect."

"What's wrong?"

"They're completely dead." Shay yanked off the goggles and shoved them back into her pocket. "Those things are never completely dead. Even when they shut off due to low power, the backup battery is enough to at least give me a little red light."

James grunted. "What does that mean?"

"That something fried it or drained even the backup power from them." She pulled her phone out of her pocket and sighed. "Of course. My phone's dead. What about yours?"

He grabbed his phone out of a belt pouch and brought it close to his face. The display was dark, and it wouldn't turn on. He shook his head.

"EMP?" James asked. "If it was, it had to be recent. The Jeep was fine."

Shay shrugged. "Maybe, or some sort of spell accomplishing the same thing." She groaned. "I was thinking we could at least use the thermal mode on the goggles. No thermal on the goggles and no drone support means we're blind here, and this storm doesn't look like it's gonna let up anytime soon. Heather said the same thing."

James marched over to the door of the nearest building, which was a glorified shed, from the looks of it. He unlatched the door and threw it open, half-expecting Brotherhood men to ambush him. He grunted when he realized the headlamp had also died.

*Should have expected that.*

A single high window allowed a small amount of light in, although given the darkening skies and advanced hour, it wouldn't be long until the building was pitch-black inside. Dusty crates filled with discolored screws sat in the corner, but there was nothing else inside. No blood, no half-eaten cultists, and no Wendigos.

James motioned her inside. "Let's talk in here," he shouted.

Shay followed him in. She shook herself and patted some of the snow coating her parka off before closing the door with a clang. She pulled her ring off, and her glow faded.

"Of course." Shay reached up and yanked off her headlamp. "Fucking perfect. I hadn't even noticed. I guess we could go back to the Jeep and grab some of the flares or the lantern. Not the first time I've had to deal with this kind of crap on a job."

James shook his head. "Don't need them yet. Probably should save them for if we get stuck here overnight."

"Good thinking." Shay leaned against a wall and nodded. "Good thing our guns, knives, and swords don't require power. We should assume the sonic grenades are useless, but the frags should still be fine. Might have an issue getting out of here after we finish up with the Brotherhood and the Wendigo."

"Nah. If we kill the wizard, the spell should go away, right?"

"If it's an ongoing thing." Shay shrugged. "If it's more an EMP, then our gear is already toast. I, for one, don't plan on walking back to Calgary."

James grunted. "Once the storm clears up, Peyton and Heather can send someone our way."

"True enough. You're right." She slid down the wall to sit. "Is Whispy okay?"

He could still feel emotions leaking off the amulet, so he'd assumed the amulet was fine, but it wouldn't hurt to check.

*You okay?* James thought.

*Operational levels are normal,* the amulet responded, the thought flavored with a hint of irritation. *Power level insufficient for advanced transformation.*

*Yeah, yeah. Don't need that yet.*

*Find enemies. Kill enemies. Adapt and achieve primary directive.*

James nodded. "He's fine, and annoying like normal. Don't know if he's immune to EMPs or if they've never worked on him."

"Who knows? Alien technology could be based on principles we can't even begin to understand. Might as well be magic." Shay frowned. "Question is what we're going to do in the meantime. The Professor's information wasn't clear on how many Brotherhood might be here."

James clenched and unclenched his fists a few times. "Don't really give a fuck. The magical poison shit was probably their best attack. Now we just need to worry about the wizard. He might have a few tricks, but if he was a badass, he wouldn't hide behind a cult."

Shay shrugged. "Maybe he likes having people to boss around. For all we know, he called down the blizzard."

"The Professor's information didn't say anything about the guy having that kind of power."

"But he does have an artifact that can increase power. I don't know. Just running the possibilities." Shay frowned and crossed her arms. "I'm more worried about the Wendigo. We also don't know if there is more than one. If we sit here the Brotherhood might come to us, or the Brotherhood might run now that they're being attacked, and the creature itself might be dangerous."

*Find new enemy,* Whispy sent. *Kill enemy. Adaptational potential high.*

James ignored the amulet. "It's just ripping people open. Not a big deal. Brotherhood can't run. They don't have portal magic. The blizzard's gonna keep them here, and if they did the anti-electronics spell, they've fucked up any cars they might have taken to escape. Maybe they will stroll into this shed and I can take the rest of them out, then I can go finish off the Wendigo. Claws? Big deal. I've already adapted to that sort of attack."

She snorted. "Like you were adapted to magical poison punches? You can't be certain what you'll face."

"Haven't lost yet." James shrugged. "Must be doing something right."

"Spoken like a true man. If you hadn't had healing potions, you might have been killed."

"Not gonna apologize for being prepared."

Shay shook a finger at him. "You're the one who said you weren't even sure it was a Wendigo."

"Maybe it is, maybe it isn't, but it's killing people like one. Doesn't really matter if it's a bounty hunter, a wizard, or a Wendigo. They'll all die if you rip their heads off."

"There's a certain simple elegance to that idea." Shay sighed and slapped a fist against the metal wall, the sound echoing in the empty storage shed. "This is so fucking annoying. Could be worse, though. At least we didn't have to go underwater."

A loud but distant noise cut through the howling wind. A roar.

"Did you hear that?" James asked. "Sounded like our bounty-poaching monster to me."

Shay nodded. "Don't know what a Wendigo sounds like, but probably a lot like that."

"He's probably getting pretty cocky now. He's carved through all those cultists and thinks he's big shit. Good time to take him out."

Whispy Doom's excitement leaked into James' thoughts.

"Maybe." Shay frowned and shrugged.

"That roar proves he's still around," James rumbled. "While we're sitting in here, that thing's stealing my bounties. I need to go out there and finish him off. At least then I know I can get rid of the rest of the Brotherhood myself."

"That's not a good plan. I know you like to keep things simple, but reality isn't always simple, James, and I don't want to have to explain to Alison how I let her dad die because he was stubborn." Shay shook her head. "I figured that in a worst-case scenario we could use the AR goggles, but they're dead. Zero visibility means you're waiting for that thing to gut you. Even if you think you've adapted to its attacks already, you can't kill something you can't see. It's a fucking cannibal spirit native to this area. I'm sure it's got white fur, or at least can blend in with the snow."

"Sure. If it *is* a Wendigo."

Shay stared at him. "The man it ripped up thought it was."

James grunted. "Doesn't matter. All that matters is if the sonofabitch thinks I'm easy prey. He'll come to me, and I'll take him out." He slammed his fist into his palm. "Unless he takes my head off in one blow he won't win, and judging by the bodies we've found, that's not his style."

"I can't believe you're basing your whole strategy on the

fact that he only mutilated people instead of ripping their heads off." Shay groaned and ran a hand down her face. "Seriously?"

"Going off the available evidence." James shrugged. "That seems like the smart play."

"Just saying, if it can't gut you, it could bury you out there, or you could end up wandering away from the refinery." Shay shook her head. "It's a bad idea. You're tough, James, but even *you* need to see what you're fighting and where you are. We have no idea how long the storm will last."

James grunted. "We can't just sit here while it steals and eats all the bounties." He blinked. "Wait. I've got an idea."

"Other than, march into a blizzard to hunt a Wendigo?"

"Nah, that's still the plan. I just thought of a better way to do it."

Shay's incredulity was obvious on her face. "And what is that?"

"Remember the pay-per-view?"

Shay stared at him, her mouth open. "Are you seriously trying to remind me of something that pissed me off while we're in a storage shed in Alberta during a blizzard? If the Wendigo or the cult doesn't take you out, maybe I will."

James shrugged. "The pay-per-view isn't important; it's how I took down the sniper that's important. Remember?"

Shay shot up, her eyes wide. "Yeah, the biological AR that altered your vision." She smiled. "You clever sonofabitch. Thermal vision?

He nodded.

"We can't be sure if the Wendigo would show up," Shay

replied, "but at least the cultists would. Are you sure you can get the amulet to give you thermal vision?"

"Time to find out. Give me a sec."

*Whispy,* James thought. *Alter my eyes so I can see body heat.*

*Acknowledged. Minor decrease in defensive efficiency required.*

*Don't care. Just do it.*

*Acknowledged. Find enemy. Kill enemy. Adapt and achieve primary directive.*

Pain exploded in James' eyes and he fell to one knee, squeezing his eyes shut and gritting his teeth.

"Shit," Shay yelled. "What's wrong?"

"Fuck."

"James?" Shay rushed over to him.

The pain ebbed, and James opened his eyes. A bright orange-red form stood in front of him, the background in shades of blue. A few seconds passed before James realized the colors overlaid the inside of the shed and Shay.

"I'm fine," he rumbled. He waved a hand in front of his face. He was running a few degrees hotter than Shay from what he could tell, likely from the amulet's bonding. "It worked. I've got thermal vision."

Shay laughed. "Hope the bad guys don't blind you with a fireball." She clapped once. "Okay, Queen Pessimism is gone, and the Empress of Ass-kicking has returned. Let's go find ourselves some cultists and a Wendigo." She patted her sword. "If guns or your fists don't work, we can use this before having to rely on your hate ray."

"Hate ray?" James frowned.

"Yeah, you know, you get all super-pissy and change.

Hate ray's catchier than hate and anger beam or whatever." Shay shrugged.

"Fine. You can call it a hate ray." James shook his head. "But I'm gonna do this alone anyway."

"Is this about you being worried about losing control and hurting me?" Shay snorted. "It's fine. You've transformed several times and kept your ass-kicking focused on the enemy. I'm not worried."

"That's not it. I need to do this alone."

"What the fuck?" Shay glared at him. "You expect me to sit here while you wander into a blizzard to take on the rest of a cult and a damned Wendigo by yourself?"

He shrugged. "Yeah, basically."

"Did Whispy rewire your brain when he gave you thermal vision?" Shay crossed her arms and frowned. "Why the hell should I sit this out?"

James shook his head. "You said it yourself. You can't fight what you can't see." He pointed to his eyes. "I can see heat now, but it's not like I can send the information to you. If you go out there with me, as badass as you are, you'll be a liability. If I knew you could see the enemy I wouldn't worry, but in a blizzard? There's no way I'm gonna have you go out there and offer yourself up as a snack."

Shay gritted her teeth and looked down. "I can… Maybe… *Shit.*" She slammed a fist against the wall. "Wait." She pointed at his chest. "You used that thing to stun me before. Maybe it can give *me* thermal vision, too?"

James furrowed his brow. "Huh. Hadn't thought of that."

*Whispy,* he sent, *can you alter Shay's vision?*

*Insufficient biological matrix combinability for permanent functional modification. Limited attacks available.*

James shook his head. "No go. Probably only works on whatever the fuck I am."

Shay sighed and nodded. "It was worth a shot. Fine. As much as it pisses me off to sit here while you go and have all the fun, I'll do it." She waved a fist at him. "But you better be careful. Remember what I said: the cult or whatever, they won't be shit, but I'm still worried about the Wendigo. Judging by other magical creatures we've both fought, you can't depend on it just being strong. Don't underestimate it or assume you'll be immune to its attacks. You might not be able to beat it using conventional means."

James chuckled and patted the amulet underneath his shirt. "If I need them, I've got unconventional means."

*Power level insufficient for advanced transformation.*

*Not helping, even if she can't hear you.*

James grunted.

Shay unbuckled her sword belt and held it up. "Take this. You don't have to give in to the Dark Side or whatever for it to work."

"No. There's still a chance you might get attacked while you're waiting. I've got Whispy, and you need the sword in case the Wendigo or the wizard shows up. Either of those will take more than a few shots from an AK to put down."

Shay sighed and wrapped the belt around her waist again. "Fine. Finish this shit. I can't even play on my phone. Maybe I should start bringing a paperback every time I go on a job. This sucks." She blew out a breath. "Kill that damned Wendigo fast."

# CHAPTER SIXTEEN

James slammed the shed door shut behind him and surveyed the area. A group of red-orange blobs moved on the other side of the central refinery building. More Brotherhood. Judging by the pattern he'd encountered so far, the Wendigo would be where the cultists were.

*Losing focus here. Fuck it. I'll just kill everyone and everything, and that'll make shit simple again.*

He trudged through the snow, ignoring the harsh wind blasting his face, the faintest hints of chill touching his amulet-enhanced skin.

James spared a glance behind him to make sure Shay wasn't following before continuing his march. No matter what else happened on this job, he needed to make sure she was safe and not blindly following him into the storm.

The blobs became human outlines as he closed—several of them. They rushed with quick movements around a central point, punching and kicking something he couldn't make out at a distance. Whatever they were fighting was the same temperature as the air around it.

*Shit. So much for the thermal vision.*

The arm flew off one man, and his body collapsed to the ground. Another man, struck by a force still invisible to James, rolled across the ground. He stopped moving.

*Have to give it to these Brotherhood assholes; they don't know when to give up. Too bad they are such twisted fucks.*

James continued pushing through the deep snow with a grunt. The cultists continued to dodge, along with striking at something the bounty hunter couldn't make out in the frigid maelstrom.

As badly as he still wanted to deny it, one strong candidate presented itself. The evidence he'd collected suggesting that a bounty hunter or normal shifter was responsible for the Brotherhood attacks was circumstantial.

He grunted.

*Shay was right. It* is *a fucking Wendigo, or at least some stupid-ass magical monster. Might need something a little more badass than my gun to take it out.*

*Insufficient power for advanced transformation,* Whispy sent.

*Yeah, yeah. I'm more irritated than pissed, I get it.*

Something loud and inhuman bellowed, the sound cutting through the wind.

*Need to get to him before he runs off again. Why does he keep going after the Brotherhood? Focused on their magic, maybe?*

"Stop running, fucker," James muttered.

He rushed forward, charging through the snow on the ground and the flakes swirling around him. More men lost their limbs as he moved close enough to discern the rough outline of a massive white creature. The monster was surrounded by four cultists, and the remains of several others littered the ground.

*You fuckers just can't win.*

*Engage and kill new enemy,* Whispy ordered.

*That's the plan. Just need to get to him while he's distracted.*

James pushed closer to the battle and grunted. Standing on two feet, the creature was over ten feet tall. That confused James, since the first building he'd entered hadn't had that high a ceiling, and the door was barely tall enough for him to pass.

*Flexible bastard, I guess.*

White fur covered the hulking monster, and its thick arms and hands were tipped with white claws. A squat nose sat in the center of his broad head, but the glowing blue eyes and mouth filled with sharp teeth drew the most attention.

*Huh. So that's what a Wendigo looks like. Looks like what I figured a Yeti does, too. Maybe they're related.*

Two of the Brotherhood charged the creature from opposite sides, both landing solid glowing punches. The Wendigo roared and raked one of the men with its claws, sending him to the ground with a scream, his blood pooling beneath him. The other cultist ducked an attack and spun, perhaps to flee. His enemy opened his back with a powerful swipe and the man pitched forward, landing face-first in the snow with his blood spraying everywhere.

James frowned. Normally, seeing crazed cultists getting taken out would have pleased him, but the more he thought about the situation, the more irritated he grew.

*No, this can't go down like this.*

Years earlier in his career, he'd gone down to take out several level-four bounties in San Juan, Puerto Rico. When he'd kicked in the door to their safe house, he'd found them dead, all drained of blood. Locals claimed a Chupacabra had killed them, but when James delivered the bodies to the local authorities, they only paid him a portion of the reward based on the various "active effort" laws designed to ensure bounty hunters weren't always undercutting each other.

James had never thought much about the laws before or after because he never considered poaching bounties, but now they might cost him his money.

He had hoped that if another bounty hunter were hunting the cult, he could at least bag the head wizard and get most of the reward, but if a monster killed everyone, the whole situation could turn into Puerto Rico all over again.

*Fucking Wendigo. Couldn't you have waited one damned day?*

*Shit. I didn't even think to check and see if there's a bounty on a Wendigo anywhere in Canada. This thing has to be worth money. The Brotherhood can't be the only people it has fucked with.*

James continued his advance. The only spots of heat he could see on the Wendigo were from the fresh blood of its victims splattered on its fur and face. The monster's temperature matched the environment exactly, and he was fortunate Whispy's thermal vision modification worked as an overlay rather than a replacement or he'd be fighting blind.

Another cultist tried a kick, but the Wendigo caught his leg and ripped out his throat with its other hand. The final surviving cultist backed away, his eyes wide. The monster pounced on the screaming man. Two quick claw strikes shredded his face and neck before the Wendigo lifted him and bit into his neck.

*Damn, the thing's faster than I would have thought, and... Well, fuck, he is going to eat all of them.*

James scrubbed a hand down his face.

*Give me normal vision. Want my defenses maxed out for this, and you said that shit cost me a little.*

*Adjusting. Kill new enemy. Adapt and achieve primary directive.*

James hissed as his eyes burned, but the pain was nowhere near the intensity of when he'd activated the thermal vision. He took a few deep breaths and stalked toward the hungry monster while he checked out the bodies, wondering if the Wendigo had already made the trip pointless.

They all looked like normal Brotherhood cult members. Their leader must still be hiding in one of the other buildings, although at the rate of loss, he doubted there were many actual cultists left.

*That urn has to be somewhere, at least. Not like that fucker could eat it. Whole thing's turning more into a tomb raid than a bounty hunt.*

"You stupid piece of shit," James shouted. "You want a real fight? Fight me."

The Wendigo spun his way, the dead cultist still in hand. The monster tossed the half-eaten body to the crimson-stained ground and roared.

"Fuck that shit." James slapped a hand on his chest. "This was supposed to be fucking relaxing. I wouldn't give two shits about you killing a bunch of cultist fucks, but you're messing with the entire reason I came here. I better not have come to Nowhere-fucking-Alberta in the middle of a blizzard for no damned reason. I could have been back in fucking LA walking my dog in sixty-degree temperatures and planning for my next PFW competition. If I came all the way up here to watch you eat people, I'm gonna be very, very pissed off. And when I'm pissed-off, I like to get rid of the shit that's pissing me off."

His heart rate kicked up, and he flexed his hands. What if the disruption field from earlier had nothing to do with Shay and him? Maybe it was part of a desperate cult defense against the monster? The timing fit.

James brushed snow off his face as he brooded about the Wendigo choosing to attack the cult shortly before his arrival. If the monster had killed them all a day before, the Canadian government would have likely noticed, given that they had the area under surveillance, and rescinded the bounty. He could have waited for a nice his-and-hers ass-kicking down in Mexico.

*Is this bad luck, or is this fucker targeting me for some reason? It's just a fucking monster.*

James gritted his teeth. Maybe Heather was on to more than he realized. He'd assumed it was Canadian intelligence or the mercenaries trying to watch him in cyberspace, but if someone was watching him and also working with magical forces, they might have been able to direct a monster his way, if only to screw with him. A convenient portal or straight conjuring, even.

*More fuckers out there want a piece of me? They thought they could win if it was just Shay and me in the middle of a job? Screw them. At least He Who Hunts had the balls to come at me in LA instead of trying to ambush me in the middle of nowhere.*

James let out a low growl of irritation. His eyes narrowed on the massive monster several yards away. Whatever the reason, the Wendigo was the source of all his current irritation.

*Yes,* Whispy sent. *Anger. Hatred.*

The Wendigo didn't move or run. Instead, it sniffed the air as its glowing blue eyes stared at James.

"This was supposed to be a fun little thing for Shay and me," James yelled. "To get it out of our systems. Then I had to come up here in this fucking snow to take out these cultists, and now I don't even know if I'm gonna get full money because of some piece-of-shit cannibal spirit-monster who couldn't leave well enough the fuck alone and is the weapon in some asshole's trap."

He waited, glaring at the monster as if daring it to charge him and prove its might. The vicious creature, which had killed and ripped apart so many men, didn't move, roar, or try to talk. It continued staring at him as if sizing him up.

*Shay didn't tell me if this thing can talk, but probably not. Who's the real monster now, fucker?*

*Engage enemy for additional adaptation,* Whispy demanded. *Kill enemy.*

Even a bloodthirsty alien amulet gave good advice now and again.

James yanked out his .45. "This shit ends now. I don't even give a shit if there's no bounty for you. You have probably been eating people for a long time now. Go back to hell, asshole. If someone sent you, they should know I'll find them eventually and fuck them up, just like I did the Harriken, the Council and the Drow queen. People should stop fucking with me, already."

The creature took a single step forward and let out a low growl, blood staining its lips and the fur around its mouth.

"Finally ready to fight, fucker?" James sneered and fired three quick shots into the creature's chest. The Wendigo jerked back, but no wound or obvious blood appeared. If the monster hadn't reacted, James wouldn't have known he'd hit it.

The Wendigo roared and thrust its arms to its side. That had to mean something.

"That hurt, huh?" James aimed at the monster's head. "How about this, then?" He pulled the trigger. The swirling snow made it hard to see, but he was sure a small hole appeared for a second before sealing. "One thing I miss about the Harriken is how easy those fuckers were to kill."

James grunted and emptied his clip into the Wendigo's head. This time the assault produced obvious holes, but they disappeared too quickly to do anything more than inconvenience the monster. No blood of any color leaked out of the wounds.

*Damn it. Maybe this thing really* is *some sort of spirit, or he just regenerates damned fast.*

*Engage and kill enemy,* Whispy demanded. *Adaptation potential high.*

Shay crept into his thoughts.

*Shit. If I go down for whatever reason, that thing might go after her. I can't mess around.*

*Engage and kill enemy,* his amulet insisted. *Other tactical considerations irrelevant.*

James snorted.

*It wasn't all that long ago you were trying to guilt-trip me about my friends, and now fuck 'em, huh? Well, fuck you. I'm taking this thing down, finding the damned cult leader, taking his head, and getting my fucking reward. Then I'm gonna go back to somewhere you only read about snow in books.*

James ejected his empty magazine, yanked a magazine containing anti-magic bullets out of his tactical vest, and slapped it into his gun.

"Eat this shit and see how you like it, you big furry asshole, and thanks for making me waste money." James put another tight three-round burst into the monster's chest with a satisfied grin.

*What the fuck?*

The smile faded. No gaping wounds followed, nothing more than a quick jerk from the Wendigo. The anti-magic bullets hadn't accomplished anything more than his conventional rounds. So, he'd both managed to waste money and do nothing to weaken his enemy.

The Wendigo didn't roar or bellow. Its huge chest rose and fell as it stared at James as if waiting for him to make another move.

"You're more than just some rampaging monster, aren't you? And here I figured those Brotherhood fucks were just being stupid." James shook his head. "Why don't you come at me, already? Let's see what you got, if you're so tough."

With a final echoing bellow, the Wendigo loped off with no sign of injury.

"Damn it," James shouted. "And now you're fucking running away? This shit isn't over."

He yanked his feet out of the snow and tromped after the white enemy disappearing into the snowy haze filling the area. He fired again, but if he hit, it didn't slow his enemy.

"Should have taken the fucking sword," he muttered and holstered his gun.

The creature pulled away, and James' heart sped up. Something was off. If he couldn't hurt the creature even with anti-magic bullets, why was it running away?

No way was he letting it escape.

*This thing is just fucking with me; trying to stall me maybe. Some piece-of-shit monster comes in here and starts fucking with my bounties and makes me spend longer in the middle of a fucking blizzard. I'm gonna fucking tear that thing apart.*

James ground his teeth. Maybe it was an unfortunate coincidence or a magical conspiracy. He didn't care. All he cared about was taking the monster out and making him pay for wasting his time.

*Sufficient power for advanced transformation achieved,* Whispy announced.

*Then do it.*

James growled.

Silver-green metallic tendrils shot from the amulet, stretching over his chest, back, and arm, a blade extending from atop his armored arm.

Faint surprise struck him. He'd been angry, but not

nearly as angry as the last time he'd achieved advanced mode.

*Achieve adaptation before killing enemy,* Whispy ordered.

*This thing ruined my trip and might be here just to screw with me.*

James narrowed his eyes. The sky was even darker than before. Once nightfall came, even with Whispy's help, he wouldn't be able to track down his enemy. All the more reason to kill the Wendigo soon.

*I'll fucking send it back to where it came from. Your adaptation shit is way down on the list of crap I care about right now.*

He rushed after his prey, his legs stronger, but the Wendigo was already out of sight. He almost asked Whispy to reactivate thermal vision mode before remembering it wouldn't help. The angry thoughts circulating in his head squashed his attempts to think of alternatives.

"Where are you, you sonofabitch?" he shouted, challenging the storm as much as the monster. "You'll kill all those Brotherhood assholes, but you're afraid of me?" He growled. "You stalling? Is that what this is? For what? Unless you drop a nuke on me, I'm not going down. Fucking face me already."

The bounty hunter continued stomping through the snow in the direction he'd last spotted the monster. He grinned as he caught sight of two huge footprints leading toward a huge gray storage tank. He rushed to follow the trail, even as falling snow started to fill in the prints.

*Stop running, fucker. Come on, you're supposed to be this big bad cannibal spirit of the North.*

James frowned and slowed. The snow was not piling up on or around the tank. Instead, it angled off, as if an invisible dome surrounded the entire thing. He followed the footprints until he reached the edge of the invisible field. A thin layer of melting snow surrounded the area, with higher snow drifts all around.

Footprints in the shallow inner snow layer continued from the edge of the invisible dome toward a closed round hatch at the bottom of the tank. It didn't look big enough for James to fit through, let alone the Wendigo.

"Can the fucker walk through walls? That would explain a lot."

James stomped toward the hatch, his anger almost blinding him to the fact that he wasn't having to make his way through deep snow. He sped up as he approached the tall tank.

"Stop fucking running," James shouted. "I'm here, and I'm pissed. The longer I spend here, the angrier I get."

He jogged over to a ladder leading to the roof of the tank. Half the ladder was missing, only rust and a few bolts remaining.

The Wendigo might blend into the environment, but it couldn't just disappear. The damned thing had to be around somewhere.

James grunted. If it was running, that meant it was afraid. Even if his gun didn't work, maybe the monster knew its claws and strength wouldn't work on him.

He stared at the tank. If it could walk through walls, that was the obvious hiding spot.

"Time to open this can," he rumbled and raised his blade.

# CHAPTER SEVENTEEN

Shay paced the storage shed, her heart pounding. She stopped a few times to kick at the walls, her boot's *thud* echoing in the small room.

"This is what I get for trying to reset our fucking luck," she muttered. "Now James is fighting a fucking cannibal spirit in a damned blizzard, and I'm trapped in here doing nothing. Great. Fucking great. Best his-and-hers ass-kicking ever." She threw her hands up in disgust. "Next time we'll just fly to Chernobyl and roll around in the reactor core. That'll be just as much fun."

The air on the opposite wall shimmered, and Shay snapped up her AK.

"Of course. I should have expected this."

Shay narrowed her eyes, watching the shimmering air condense into a blurry image of a woman in a dark skirt and a matching top.

She snorted. "Seriously? I don't have time for ghost bullshit right now. If you're the spirit of some sad pioneer chick or something, come back another time after we're done clearing out a cult and killing a Wendigo."

*I should be off helping James kick Wendigo ass, not dealing with this bullshit.*

The woman chuckled. "A ghost? Is that what you think I am?"

"Oh, you talk." Shay kept her gun pointed. "I've got anti-magic bullets in here, by the way, so don't think you'll be safe just because of what you are. You're not the first ghost I've run into."

In truth, she had no idea how effective the bullets might be against ghosts since she'd only had a few brief encounters with such entities, but confidence could cow supernaturals as well as normal people.

"I'm not worried," the blurry woman responded, her tone amused. A slight accent underlay her words that Shay didn't recognize, which was rare for the tomb raider. The woman crossed her arms and shook her head, although the blurriness of her face made it impossible to read her expression. "It's proven surprisingly difficult for me to contact you. I hope you appreciate the effort."

"You *aren't* a ghost, are you?" Shay narrowed her eyes.

"I never claimed such a thing, Miz Carson."

Shay slung her rifle over her shoulder. Whatever was about to happen wouldn't involve a gun battle, although she kept her hands at her sides so she could go for her sword if necessary. The *tachi* had proven its worth against a variety of magical foes, to the point she trusted it implicitly. Maybe a mistake, but she hoped it wouldn't come to that.

"How do you know who I am?" Shay asked.

The blurry woman shrugged. “Is it really a secret? I understand that it was before, but you’ve become more visible as time has gone by and you’ve let your past leak through to your present. I’m good at finding things out when I need to be. Let’s just say it’s part of my job.”

“Please.” Shay scoffed. “You don’t know shit about me. You’re bluffing.”

“Don’t I?” The woman shook her head. “You were nothing but a murderous parasite, a killer for hire. Your every action made the world a worse place. Even if you let yourself believe you were killing bad people, you were doing it at the behest of scum. You were a tool of evil and corruption. Pathetic.”

Shay’s heart rate kicked up. Even if more people knew her past than a year ago, that didn’t mean some random woman showing up in Alberta should know it.

*Fuck. This isn’t just a bluff.*

“The question is,” the blurry woman continued, “have you truly left your past behind? You hide behind the mask of the tomb raider who goes by ‘Aletheia,’ but it’s not as if you never hurt anyone on your job, now is it? I wonder if you’ve killed more people as a tomb raider than you did as a killer?”

“Fuck you. I don’t hurt innocent people, and I don’t kill people who aren’t trying to kill me.” Shay’s stomach tightened. How did the woman know so much about her?

*The accent doesn’t sound Canadian, either primary Anglophone or Quebecois. So, a witch from Europe? Who the fuck is she? Time to go on offense.*

“If you’re here to punish me for my past, bring it on,” Shay snarled. “I can sleep at night, and I’m not apologizing to some random blurry-ass woman for who I am, or was. The question is, can *you* sleep at night?"

"No." The woman laughed. "Often I can't. The demons who haunt me are far worse than you can possibly imagine, which is why I've devoted my life to protecting people from them." The blurry woman took a few steps toward Shay.

She clutched the hilt of her sword. "Don't come any closer if you don't want to die. Like I said, I don't kill people who aren't trying to kill me, but that doesn't mean I'm gonna be stupid about letting people surprise me. I still have no idea who the fuck you are."

The woman shrugged. "I'm not actually here, Miz Carson. You can't hurt me. If it sets you at ease, I've put a lot of effort into relaying this image to you so we can talk, despite the interference the Brotherhood has set up. I wanted to take this opportunity to talk to you while you're alone. I've sacrificed paying attention to another important matter just for this conversation, so I hope it ends up being useful."

"Talk about what? My past? Me killing people on tomb raids? If you're going to try to Scrooge me, don't bother. I've already turned my back on my past, and I'm fine with the way I'm living my life now." Shay kept her hand on her sword. "I don't need to be told any of that shit about my past, and I know all about the people I've screwed over. And, yes, I'll kill anyone who threatens me or those I care about. So either try to kill me or fuck off."

"You misunderstand me, but I'm happy to hear you say that," the woman replied. "Not the killing, but that you understand your past. It means you have some sense of morality left and care about someone other than yourself. That means you might actually respond to what I have to say."

Shay frowned. "Who the hell are you? You can't be with the Brotherhood. They don't allow women, and you don't sound like a person who would agree with their twisted bullshit."

The woman snorted. "They are magical parasites who squander their glorious abilities on preying on the weak. No, I'm not with the Brotherhood, and I don't care that they're dying. I'm only interested in protecting the Earth and Oriceran from those who would prey on them, and if you've truly turned your back on the past and care about others, then you should care about that too."

Shay let her hand drop from her sword. "You don't get to lecture me. I've dealt with all sorts of threats, including the Council. I've done my part, and then some. Can you say the same?"

"Yes. I do my part every day." The blurry woman turned her back and sighed. She marched over to the wall and crossed her arms before turning back around. "How much do you really know about James Brownstone?"

"Huh? What's that supposed to mean?"

"The question is easy to understand." The woman's voice sounded distorted, and her already blurred image faded for a few seconds. "Do you really know James Brownstone, Miss Carson? Can you say you do? Do you know where he comes from?"

Shay burst out laughing. "I've been fucking him. I think I know him pretty damned well."

The blurriness around the woman's face denied Shay the ability to read surprise or understanding on it.

"I see," the woman murmured. She sighed. "That's… surprising, but be that as it may, you should understand that just because he looks like a man and tests say he's a man, he's not a man. He's far, far from it."

Shay frowned. "Surprising? Why would it be… Wait. What are you getting at, exactly?"

"I know you've seen it. He's more than a mere bounty hunter. He's a violent monster. He's done well to hide it, but I know he's not just a human with a nice artifact." Venom dripped from the woman's voice. "And if you know him as well as you suspect, then you must understand that as well."

Shay swallowed. "Who the fuck are you? What do you think you know about James, you blurry bitch?"

The woman's image twisted for a moment, and an out-of-focus image of an armored James in extended advanced mode, complete with an arm blade and featureless helmet, replaced her.

Shay's stomach tightened.

*No! There's no way she knows James is an alien.*

"Are you going to deny this is what he truly is?" The image reset to the blurry vision of the woman. "A monster who pretends to be a man?"

"You're the one," Shay snarled through gritted teeth. "You're the one who sent the mercenaries after him. You're the one who fucked with Customs somehow. Who. The. Fuck. *Are*. You?"

"I did what I had to do." The woman sighed. "And you don't need to know who I am, but I find myself frustrated that now that he's used his armor, no one sees the monster Brownstone is. You've seen it yourself, yet you still are at his side." She shook her head. "Ridiculous."

Shay took a deep breath. The woman didn't sound like someone he'd fought in the past, and her constant insistence about how dangerous he was pointed to something other than merely a concerned government official.

*If I figured out that James isn't human, could somebody else have, too? Who is she? Someone from Project Ragnarok or Project Nephilim? Why bother with all this complicated bullshit instead of sending black ops types after him?*

*Maybe she's afraid of pushing James too far, which means she doesn't have all of the government on her side. I can use that against her. I have to try to gather as much information as I can so we can fight back.*

Shay shrugged. "If you know so much and you can manipulate government officials, why bother with any of this? If you think James is a unique threat, why not go tell the government bastards who have fucked with him in the past and set them after him?"

The woman gave a dark chuckle. "We all have our constraints, Miz Carson. I'm trying to help you see the danger associated with a creature like James Brownstone."

*Damn it. She* definitely *knows what he is. The way she's talking doesn't make sense otherwise.*

Shay took several deep breaths. "James has proven himself to me a lot of times. He's also proven himself to everyone else. Without James Brownstone's efforts, the Council would have continued to slaughter innocent people. If you think he's some sort of monster, explain that. He didn't need the money."

The woman sighed. "It's like the scorpion and the tortoise, Miz Carson."

"Like the fable?" Shay snorted. "Give me a fucking break. Real life doesn't work that way."

"I disagree. It works out that way far too often." The woman cut through the air with her hand. "No, you *think* you understand what he is, but you don't. Eventually, he'll turn on you, just as the scorpion stung that tortoise in the middle of the river, causing them both to die. Why? Because it's his nature."

"Bullshit. Nothing but old-school fear." Shay shook her head. "People fear what they don't understand. If thousands of years of human history didn't teach us that, then the last twenty years of Earth and Oriceran history have. I don't know what you think James' true nature is, but he's no fucking scorpion. He's a bounty hunter, not a criminal. He could have set himself up easily."

A dark laugh erupted from the blurry woman. "Can you say that without reservation? Can you say that you've never seen a dangerous darkness that made you question him for at least a second?"

"I'm no angel, and I'm not perfect." Shay shrugged. "You just got done saying I was a piece of shit, remember? Do you expect me to hate on James for not being an angel? Spare me!"

"Maybe you're not an angel, but you're not a demon either." The woman pointed at Shay. "If you continue to associate with Brownstone, you'll become a handmaiden of death. Your past as a killer will pale in comparison."

Shay laughed. "Really? 'Handmaiden of death?' I kind of like the title." She unsheathed her sword. "And if you're here trying to get into my head, that means whatever trap you set here might not work. No, you're *convinced* it's not gonna work. I don't know what kind of magic you used to lure the Wendigo here, but you know James well enough to know he might win." She shook her head. "No. More than that. You think he *is* gonna win." She marched forward. "Ha. All your little plans are going up in smoke, aren't they?"

The blurry woman sighed. "You don't understand. I wish I could tell you more, so you'd understand."

"Oh, I understand all too well. Whatever dark secrets you think you know about James, I've known for a while, and I don't care. Handmaiden of death? You're damned right. I'll kill anyone who even *thinks* about fucking with him, and it sounds a lot like you're planning to fuck with me." Shay pointed her sword at the woman. "On the off chance he doesn't win against the Wendigo, you should know that no matter where you go or where you hide, I'll devote the rest of my life to finding you and cutting your head off with this sword."

"It sounds like we're done here, Miz Carson."

"Yeah. I think so." Shay stabbed at the woman. Her sword passed right through.

The woman snorted. "I told you that I'm not really here."

"I don't have any reason to believe a single thing you've said." Shay sheathed her sword. "And I thought it was a good chance to protect James. I could have gotten lucky and taken out a dangerous threat."

"The tortoise shouldn't protect the scorpion," the woman replied. "Whatever feelings you think you're experiencing involving that creature, you should know he can't reciprocate them. You're being used; manipulated by a monster who will kill you. I can only hope you see the light before it's too late. You're too smart a woman to betray your own planet."

The image vanished.

Shay stared for a moment, wondering if the woman would come back. No doubt filtered into her mind. The woman was right. James wasn't what he appeared. Maybe he *was* a monster.

She didn't care. He was *her* monster, and she loved him.

*You better run far, far away, bitch.*

## CHAPTER EIGHTEEN

The wind weakened and the snowfall lightened, but it was still hard to see more than a few yards.

James growled.

*Tired of playing hide and go seek in this frozen wasteland.*

He let out a loud bellow and stabbed his blade into the wall of the tank. The sharp blade pierced the metal with ease, an echoing scraping sound accompanying it. He grunted, surprised, and sliced a hole with little effort. With the help of a boot, he kicked the perforated metal to the floor of the storage tank.

A faint acrid odor escaped the hole as the thud of the metal echoed in the dark tank. A moment later a bright orb of white light appeared near the top, illuminating the entire floor. James squinted and raised his blade.

A tall, pale man in a dark robe, his face covered with glyph scars, stood on the other side of the tank, a brown wand in hand and a small golden box sitting next to him.

James had wanted the Wendigo, and it had led him

here. A trap? Maybe. He didn't care. If he couldn't kill the Wendigo, he'd kill the murderous head of the cult standing in front of him.

"I thought I sensed something pass my barrier." The wizard let out a long sigh. "I suppose I should have expected this. How many monsters will be sent against us today?"

*Engage and kill enemy,* Whispy all but shouted, his thoughts tinged with glee. *Adaptation potential high.*

James glanced around the tank. The emptiness made it easy to search. The wizard and his box were the only contents. A ten-foot-tall Wendigo would have been easy to spot.

*Can it just turn invisible?*

"Not a monster, asshole, just a bounty hunter," James growled. "James Brownstone. I was looking for the Wendigo to kill it, but I was looking for you first, so I might as well kill you right now."

"Ah, the famous James Brownstone." The wizard bowed with a flourish. "I am Darian. I lead the Brotherhood of Silence."

"You mean your group of psychopaths who think they are going to become greater than God?" James narrowed his eyes. "How many people have you murdered to fuel your twisted-ass magic?"

He could see himself decapitating the wizard in his mind. His hands and arms twitched with the desire.

Darian smiled and shrugged. "Is it so wrong to explore the empowerment of the individual? We shouldn't chain ourselves to foolish, outmoded morality that weakens us.

Don't you think our creator would want us to greet him as equals?"

James grunted. "No, and it doesn't matter, because whatever weird-ass human sacrifice you're practicing isn't going to get you that kind of power. You assholes can't even handle one Wendigo. Couldn't have happened to a nicer group of assholes. My only regret is that I wasn't the one to kill you all."

Darian's mouth curled into a smile. "Ah, yes, the Wendigo." He clucked his tongue. "But you're not the type of man who would summon a creature like that to aid you. Interesting. I suspected something planned, but now that I see our current foe, that means there was an unfortunate confluence of events this day."

*What the fuck is wrong with this asshole?*

*Engage the enemy,* Whispy suggested. *Kill the enemy.*

James kept flexing and stretching out his clawed hand. He needed to bury that blade in an enemy soon.

"You don't even give a fuck, do you?" James snorted. "You twisted piece of shit."

"About what? The dead men?" Darian shook his head. "The strong survive, the weak perish. That's life. That's the natural order set down by the Creator. We only follow it to its logical conclusion. A conscience is a lie. A distraction."

James raised his blade. "Well, if that's the case, maybe we should test which of us is strong and which is weak? I'll give you one chance to surrender. If you don't take it, I will kill you. I want to already."

Darian raised his wand. "We're not so different, James."

"Don't fucking call me 'James,'" the bounty hunter

snarled. "You kill innocent people just to make yourself stronger. I don't fucking do that."

The wizard shrugged. "I'm only noting that, as we both know, one makes their own morality through strength. The weak are sacrificed to improve the strong, just as you've sacrificed so many throughout your career. You say it doesn't matter because they weren't innocent, but the men you've killed…did they have any chance of victory? It's my understanding that you killed hundreds of Harriken. Even if they *were* criminals, you were nothing more than a lion among the herd."

James glared at Darian. "Give it up, fucker. I've had weird-ass Oriceran monsters in my head. Nothing you can say will fuck me up."

Irritation flowed from Whispy, whether from his lack of violence or with Darian, James didn't know. He also didn't care. His anger seemed to be growing by the second. It wasn't the out-of-control explosions of rage he'd dealt with in the past, but it was building that way, as if the amulet itself wouldn't let it fade. If he were more clear-headed, he might have bothered to ask.

"You don't understand." Darian sighed. "I'm not trying to demean you. I'm trying to praise you. Can't we come to some sort of understanding? You are a man worthy of respect, so I'm granting it to you."

"Drop the wand and surrender." James pointed his blade at the wizard. "Or you fucking die. Simple as that, asshole."

Darian pointed the wand. "It's unfortunate that your mind is so inflexible. True strength includes mental strength. Goodbye, Mr. Brownstone."

A red bolt blasted from the wand and struck James. He grimaced as a brief sensation of burning shot through his body in a wave, but his armor remained untouched; not even a slight scorch.

*Near maximum adaptation achieved. Downgrading adaptation potential. Kill current enemy and engage and kill next enemy.*

James grunted. "Is that all you got? You didn't take me down with the first shot. Now you die."

Darian shuddered, a rapturous look passing over his face. "Glorious. You are what the stories say."

"I'm gonna stab this blade through your heart." James lifted his arm.

The anger deluged him now, circulating and feeding itself, threatening to boil into an explosion of feeling.

The strange juxtaposition of Whispy's happiness intertwined with the boiling cauldron of rage.

*Can think straighter than last time I was using a blade, but I'm still fucking pissed off. I want to fucking cut that guy to pieces. Want it badly, and I can't even fucking figure out... You're doing this, aren't you? Keeping me pissed.*

*Kill the enemy,* Whispy demanded. *Achieve primary directive.*

James ground his teeth and glared at Darian.

Two more red bolts shot from the wand, this time striking James in the head. He hissed and stumbled back, some pain in his eyes, but the burning wave died before it could spread.

"I don't think you understand how impressive what you're doing is," Darian murmured. "These are not mere elemental forces. They are, for want of a better description, anti-life. Even if you can survive such a blow, it should weaken you severely, but you don't even seem bothered. It's as if you're all but immune to my magic."

The brief thought of what might have happened had James encountered Darian before the Wendigo floated into his mind, but the desire to stab the bastard smothered it. It was time to give Whispy what he wanted.

James took a thunderous step forward, the impact of his boot echoing in the tank. Another step followed.

Darian frowned. "Alas. How wasteful. So be it, James Brownstone."

A shadowy nimbus formed around the tip of the wand. It swallowed the nearby light and built in intensity over several seconds as James made his ponderous approach to the wizard.

A dark sphere blasted from the wand and struck the bounty hunter in the chest, sending him flying back. He slammed against a wall, an icy sensation spreading through his veins. Pain followed.

James hissed and collapsed to one knee. His blade scraped the cold metal floor of the tank.

*Yes.* Whispy's pleasure blasted into James' mind. *New adaptation in progress.*

James grunted and stood. The blast left a hole in his armor, jagged edges surrounding it. Tingling and numbness spread through his muscles, but he stalked toward the wizard again, intent on his death.

Darian's brow lifted. "Now I am *truly* impressed. Most would have died from a single blast. I don't understand. You're obviously using some sort of artifact, but I can't sense its magic."

Whispy's joy was infectious.

*Kill the enemy. Kill the enemy. Kill the enemy.*

"Who said anything about magic, fucker?" James rumbled. "I'm gonna fucking kill you. Whoever that Wendigo didn't kill, *I'll* kill."

Darian snorted. "You bore me, Brownstone. I was a fool to not kill you from the beginning."

Another shadow ball grew at the tip of the wand as the wizard glared at him.

James did his best to ignore the numbness and agony suffusing his body. He marched toward Darian, the amulet beaming with joy, and his mind locked on a singular goal: killing the smug motherfucker in front of him.

Darian fired at James again. Pain flared from the blast point, but this time the magic didn't launch him into the air. He put another foot forward. So close.

The wizard frowned, then murmured something under his breath and flicked his wand. Another red bolt shot out, followed by a tiny shadow sphere.

James kept moving as the wizard alternated his attacks.

*Effective maximum adaptation achieved,* Whispy announced. *Kill the enemy.*

James' vision wavered. The new attack merely stung, and his armor had already started to seal the hole created by the first shadow attack, but the chilling pain from before had spread to every part of his body. Moving his muscles required all his concentration.

Still, he marched forward.

Darian's smirk disappeared, and he raised his wand again. A shadowy curtain spread from the tool on both sides and extended to the ceiling.

"I don't know how you're still alive, Brownstone, but I can wait you out." Darian nodded and gave a nervous laugh. "The Wendigo will come. You're already wounded, and it can finish you off for me."

James stomped closer until he was only a yard from Darian, separated only by the curtain. "You know what I realized a long time ago?" His voice was more growl than words at this point. "A lot of you magic-wielding fucks use the same kind of energy for your different kinds of spells."

Darian narrowed his eyes. "You think that's some sort of brilliant insight?" He snorted. "Your mind lags behind your physical prowess, Brownstone."

"You don't get it." James stepped forward and brought back his blade-tipped arm. "Adapt to one kind of energy in an attack, adapt to it in defense."

"Spare your petty threats. Now, be a good bounty hunter and d—"

James shoved the blade through the shadow wall and pierced Darian's heart. The bounty hunter slashed a few times at the defensive spell until he'd cleared most of the visible energy near him.

With a low, cold growl, he stabbed the wizard with wild abandon, the man's blood spraying all over James' armor and face. After a moment, he clawed at the wizard with the other hand, tearing into his robe and chest.

The anger swelled in him, and he needed an outlet. A target.

He wasn't sure how long he sliced, diced, and ripped the man. The attack seemed like it'd just started, but a dismembered and shredded corpse now lay in front of him, something far more badly mauled than anything the Wendigo had left behind.

Shock and regret didn't stop the attack. He felt only the freezing agony pulsing through his whole body.

*Severe cellular damage,* Whispy reported. *Maintaining advanced mode limiting cellular regeneration. Recommend reversion and quiescence for maximum regeneration.*

*No. This shit isn't over yet.*

*Recommend external healing to preserve tactical effectiveness.*

James pulled himself away from the dead wizard, barely noticing the shadow wall had vanished or that the light spell remained. He grabbed a healing potion from his belt and yanked the stopper off.

He snapped his head toward the hole he'd made as a loud roar echoed around him.

The Wendigo stood in front of the hole. James wasn't sure if the pain was clouding his mind, but the creature looked even taller than before and was almost twice the size of the hole.

"Don't you have any bones, fucker?" James growled. "How the hell do you keep squeezing into places? Whatever." He hissed and raised his arm, despite the pain. "He's dead. It's your fucking turn."

The monster charged him, and James' clouded mind didn't register that he still had the healing potion in his hand until the Wendigo slammed into him and sent him flying.

*New adaptation in progress,* Whispy announced.

Still in his hand, the healing potion crashed against the

wall before the rest of James' body, vial shattering, the liquid splattering the wall.

James grunted and slid down the wall, shaking his head.

The Wendigo roared.

James roared back and pushed himself to his feet. He didn't care about the pain or the numbness threatening to take him back to his knees. It was time to kill the enemy.

# CHAPTER NINETEEN

S*ufficient power for extended advanced mode,* Whispy declared. *Increasing basal regeneration. Kill the enemy. Achieve primary directive.*

The armor spread over all of James' body, ripping his pants and snapping his tactical vest. Claws and another blade extended from his other hand and arm. The vest fell to the ground, the magazines and other gear clacking together. The helmet closed over his head, and his eyes adjusted to a wider field of vision. The pain and numbness from before hadn't vanished, but they faded somewhat, and his burning anger pushed them to a distant corner of his mind.

An outside observer might have trouble deciding which was worse: the faceless monster in armor with double blades and claws or the white-furred man-eating giant with glowing blue eyes.

*A monster to kill a fucking monster.* James' heart thundered, his anger and hatred stoking an ever-greater fire.

The Wendigo needed to be defeated. It needed to die at his hands.

The rage filling him wasn't mindless, but neither was it easily dismissed. It was an eager hunger for the death of his enemy, as if defeating the Wendigo would plug a wound in his soul.

A faint hint of awareness tried to push into James' mind, the realization he'd achieved this kind of anger and hatred without a direct threat to Shay or Alison. The obsession with destroying his opponent overwhelmed the slight reflection, and he refocused on how to annihilate the Wendigo, the implications of his earlier thoughts lost.

The Wendigo backed up and circled James slowly as if seeking a weakness in his defenses. He resisted the urge to rush and slash it. The creature might be powerful, but he now had full armor. It would come to him, and he would take his opportunity then. He would end the threat.

*Kill the enemy,* Whispy sent. *Kill the enemy.*

James grunted in response. Killing the enemy wouldn't be enough. He wanted to destroy the enemy; reduce the enemy to dust.

The Wendigo charged and crashed into James again. The force of the blow knocked him against the wall again with a loud thud. The impact stung but did no lasting damage.

The bounty hunter's responding growl was loud, the helmet amplifying the sound. The Wendigo snarled and raised its claws.

James leapt into the air, the high ceiling of the tank allowing him to reach a good height. As he dropped toward the Wendigo, he aimed at the monster's chest. The force of the attack shoved the weapons straight through, no resistance and no cracking of bones. Something was unsatisfying about that.

"Die," James yelled. "Die, die, *die*."

The Wendigo backhanded James and the blow sent him spinning through the air before he crashed to the ground. He jumped back to his feet, expecting a stumbling enemy who was fighting off death, but the monster stood there, defiant. The damned creature wasn't even bleeding.

James let out a deep, long growl. The Wendigo responded in kind.

His opponent rushed at James again, but this time streams of crimson energy flowed over its claws. James' rage-clouded mind barely took note of the sudden change in the enemy's primary weapon until the Wendigo's claws raked his armor, ripping past the silver-green exterior and into the hardened flesh below. Pain exploded from James' chest as he stumbled back.

The Wendigo roared.

*New adaptation in progress,* Whispy reported, its joy rippling in James' mind.

His blood dripped to the bare metal floor of the tank. The new hole in the armor began to close as the Wendigo swiped again in two quick attacks. This time, James met the attack with an upward slice of his blade. He caught the Wendigo in its shoulder. The blade passed through as easily as it had during his jump attack, not meeting any hard obstacles, as if the creature had no bones. He jerked up, cutting with the blade.

The Wendigo's arm flew off and hit the floor. Smooth

and gray, the separated shoulder didn't show any signs of blood—or muscle or bone.

James paused, the sight dampening his current bloodlust for a few seconds.

His enemy took advantage of the momentary confusion to rake at James with its remaining arm, and the blow caught his side. Although the glowing claws pierced the top layer of armor, they didn't reach his chest; Whispy's adaptation was doing its work.

James hissed and stabbed both blades into the chest of the Wendigo. The creature backed up with a roar, the wounds closing without any blood. The separated arm remained on the ground, unmoving. The great cannibal spirit of the North might be able to regenerate, but it wasn't invulnerable.

The bounty hunter grunted and shook his head, some of the pain from the previous attacks catching up to him. Even in his rage, he understood the monster was too close for him to use his energy cannons because of their charging time, but his blades weren't accomplishing much besides forcing the enemy back.

Whispy flooded his mind with a familiar demand: *Kill enemy. Achieve greater adaptation for primary directive.*

The combatants circled each other. The Wendigo might look and roar like a beast, but its tactics revealed a careful creature. It'd run from James, baited him while picking off the Brotherhood cultists. It'd even waited for him to fight and kill the wizard, as if it knew he'd be weakened. Not just intelligence then, but caution born of fear. That could be used.

James' foot bumped into something soft. His expanded

range of vision let him catch a hint of Darian's corpse at his feet. He'd forgotten about the man he'd killed not all that long ago, a dangerous foe who was now just another obstacle in his latest battle.

He punted the corpse against a wall. It crunched and slid down.

The Wendigo sprang at him, its claws now glowing yellow, the change suggesting another reason for the delay. James threw up an arm to catch the Wendigo's blow. A blast of spiraling yellow energy discharged from the claws and spread through James. His muscles seized for a second, and pain flared everywhere. His vision swam, and his stomach churned.

The monster swung its claws toward James' neck, but he slammed an armored foot into its chest. The blow knocked the creature across the tank. Its massive form collided with the metal of the wall hard enough to leave a shallow dent.

*Adaptation in progress,* Whispy reported. *Severe neurological damage sustained. Potential link disruption possible. Continuing regeneration.*

Despite the warning, the amulet all but vomited happiness into James' mind. It twisted and mixed with his own anger, dulling his perception of his pain. If he wasn't dead, he could still win, and he was far from dead.

*I will kill this fucker,* he thought.

Yes, Whispy responded. *Kill, kill, kill.*

The Wendigo roared, and James answered with his own bellow, their noises echoing and overlaying each other in the large hollow metal cylinder.

The residual throbbing pain from the Wendigo's last

attack contrasted with the fading numbness from Darian's efforts. James' armor now lacked any signs of damage. Even if he was hurt, he still had his limbs and was regenerating. The only problem was that his enemy possessed similar resilience.

James let out a low growl and jumped higher than before. He twisted in flight as he passed Darian's light ball near the roof. When he reached the top, he pushed off hard with his feet, launching himself straight toward the Wendigo, his arms to his sides. He crossed the blades at the last moment, decapitating the creature before his heavy armored body crashed into the headless corpse and pinned it to the ground.

The furry head flew through the air and bounced off a wall. There was still no sign of blood. If it were a spirit, maybe decapitation wouldn't be enough, but whatever its true nature, the Wendigo had a physical body and made physical attacks, which suggested a physical solution might work.

James slammed his blades into the body again, cutting and piercing it. This time the holes didn't seal themselves, but there was still no bleeding. A quick cut removed the other arm. He followed up with the legs. He roared as he finished mincing the Wendigo, not a single bone or drop of blood visible during the violent process.

That had to be enough. He'd destroyed the body. The creature couldn't be immortal. Even He Who Hunts fell after enough damage.

James stumbled back, growling low under his breath, the hatred swirling in his mind not satisfied with the lack of a clear death.

Thin gray lines shot from each Wendigo piece toward the others, including the arm and head that were farther away.

James grunted and rushed over to the body. A few more hacks separated the gray lines, but additional ones shot out from the pieces. Both of his arms rose, and he prepared to fire his energy cannon. If cutting and slicing wouldn't work, incineration was a good option.

*Adaptation and sampling complete,* Whispy reported. *Nanoresonance determined. Initiate direct contact for disruption of enemy. Further adaptation potential minimum. Kill enemy.*

James stood there as the chunks of the Wendigo pulled back together and merged, his every instinct screaming at him to destroy the enemy, but the strange suggestion from Whispy cut through the miasma of hate in his mind. It was almost as if the angrier he became, the more he wanted to listen to the amulet.

He dropped to one knee and slapped both clawed hands into the two largest remaining pieces of the Wendigo. Green sparks flowed around the back of his blades, swirling and building in speed and intensity like they did before an energy cannon shot. A few seconds later, a wave of energy shot from his hands to the walls and roof of the tank.

The Wendigo pieces started smoking. James stood and backed away. The smoking stopped, and the pieces melted into a dull gray pool of viscous liquid.

James waited, his breathing shallow, for the monster to rise from the pool, but the anger fueling him waned with each passing second. The pool rippled at the touch of the Albertan wind blowing through the hole James had made, but the Wendigo who had so stubbornly refused to die now stubbornly refused to return from death.

His helmet retracted and James took another step back, gritting his teeth at the residual pain throughout his body. He stared down at the gray liquid, his mind struggling to comprehend what had just happened. The life-or-death struggle might be finished, but it'd left far too many questions to ignore.

The rest of his armor retracted.

*Reverting extended advanced mode transformation for maximum regeneration. External healing unnecessary.*

James grunted and staggered. He shook his head, his balance off and pain pulsing through every part of his body. He blinked several times.

*What the fuck was that? What did I just fight?*

*Contact sampling consistent with advanced nanoform,* Whispy responded.

*And what the fuck is an advanced nanoform?*

*Adaptive nanite collective. Engagement with enemy resulted in advanced adaptation.*

James grunted.

*Nanites? Like robots?*

*Adaptative nanite collective.*

James shook his head.

*But it's a magical creature, isn't it? Cannibal spirit or some shit?*

*Contact sampling and adaptation are not consistent with previously sampled magical attacks. Extremely low probability of magical nature. Useful adaptations gained, advancing unit toward primary directive.*

*And what the fuck is your primary directive?*

*Find new enemies. Engage and kill new enemies. Adapt and achieve primary directive. Entering quiescence for maximum regeneration.*

James grunted and looked down. His clothes were shredded, and Whispy had once again failed to explain his primary directive.

*Is that fucker actively hiding it from me, or am I just not understanding? I couldn't understand what he was saying to me for most of my life, so it may just be a communications thing. He's coming through when it counts.*

James scrubbed a hand over his face. Nothing about what had happened made sense, even to a man who had previously fought strange chaos monsters and telepathic Oriceran monsters in Japanese forests. Why would a Wendigo made up of little robots show up in nowhere-fucking-Alberta to attack him in the middle of a fight with a death cultist?

"This shit was about as far from relaxing as you can get," James muttered. He stomped over to the golden box and opened the lid. A gold and silver urn was inside. "At least I don't have to hunt for the artifact. *Fuck*, this was annoying. Hope the Professor appreciates this."

The pool of nanites hissed, and James grunted and spun toward it. The Wendigo didn't rise again. A pungent odor rose from the pool as it evaporated.

James frowned and grabbed the box. He backed toward the hole in the wall as the pool shrank, the harsh smell growing more intense.

*Self-destruction, or just what happens when nanites die? Don't know, and damn, I wish I could say I didn't care.*

He shook his head. It was time to get back to Shay.

# CHAPTER TWENTY

Shay leaned against the wall, staring at the shed door. She'd been warring with herself. The appearance of Little Miss Blurry had left her heart thumping louder than the howling blizzard's winds.

*Whoever that bitch was, this whole thing was a giant trap. Should I go find James? Damn it, with the storm, I'll just be a liability. If only my fucking AR goggles were working.*

*But it's not like I've never had to navigate without a toy. If I stick to my AK, it won't hurt him if I fire blindly into the storm.*

She groaned. "What the fuck am I thinking?" she muttered. "I need a better plan than to stumble around in a storm and blindly fire, hoping I only hit the enemy."

Her gaze dipped to her sword. She should have insisted James take it. It'd already helped him several times, and with a strange monster lurking around, it would have been good insurance.

She gritted her teeth. Whispy Doom was good, but the amulet wasn't a reliable weapon. A reliable weapon didn't care how you felt. You fired or swung it, and it did its job.

*How much is that thing capable of? Energy beams, blades that can cut through magic? If James got pissed enough, could he nuke something?*

She rubbed the back of her neck and swallowed, her stomach tightening.

*James was raised by good men. What the fuck would have happened if some twisted-ass cultists like the Brotherhood had found him instead of Father McCartney and Father Thomas?*

Shay let out a dark chuckle and murmured to herself, "They'd probably make a new level-seven bounty category or have to nuke him. He's been exposed to all sorts of energy and forces already. A nuke's just a scaled-up version of a lot of that: radiation, thermal, and shit." She laughed. "I wonder if he could take a nuke? Doubt he'll volunteer for the experiment, and now I'm talking to myself. I've gone crazy already, and I've only been in the blizzard for a few hours. Damn. LA's made me soft."

Something thudded against the door, and Shay ripped the AK off her shoulder and pointed the gun at the door.

"Looks like someone's making the decision for me." Shay narrowed her eyes and backed farther away from the door. She set her gun to automatic fire. At this range, it'd be hard to miss, and she needed to force her enemies back so she could escape the shed.

Shay took a slow, deep breath, her eyes locked on the door, her heart thundering.

*Don't worry, James. You do what you need to do, and I'll do what I need to do. I'm not dying in some fucking shed in Alberta.*

The door flew open, harsh wind and snow flowing into the shed. James stood in the doorway, a frown on his face and his clothes a ripped and hole-filled mess. His tactical vest was gone.

Shay activated the safety, lowered her weapon, and let out a sigh of relief. Her man stepped inside with a box under one arm and slammed the door shut.

"Looks like you got in a fight or two," Shay offered with a smile and slung her rifle over her shoulder. "I hope this is the part where you say, 'You should see the other guy.'"

"Yeah." James grunted. "The head of the Brotherhood is dead." He set the box in front of the door. "The urn's in there."

Shay grinned. "Good. Even if the Canadian government tries to fuck with you over the bounties, at least we have this. Did *you* kill the guy, or was it the Wendigo?"

"It was me. He was an annoying piece of shit. Gave me a big speech."

"Oh, more dick-measuring contests?" Shay smirked. "I worry about them when I'm not there to end them with a good blade or bullet."

James shook his head. "Nah. Fucker thought he could convince me to join his dumbass cult. Wendigo showed up right after that. I killed it too, but it…" He grimaced. "It wasn't a Wendigo."

Shay blinked. "Wasn't a Wendigo? Shifter after all? Or some magic-using type with an artifact?"

"Not magical at all."

"Huh? You saying it's some other kind of cryptid?" She laughed. "You saying it actually was a Yeti and not a Wendigo?"

"No. I'm saying it was a bunch of nanites." James shrugged.

Shay laughed. When he didn't laugh back, she stared at him. "Wait a minute. You're serious?"

"Fucker shredded me through my armor. Yeah, I'm serious. Adaptive nanite collection, properly described as a nanoform."

Shay shook her head. She understood the words coming out of James' mouth, but they didn't sound like something he'd come up with himself. What the hell had happened?

"Nanites?" She sighed. "Let me be clear: when you say nanites, you mean little robots? If I'm following you, you're claiming a group of little robots pretended to be a Wendigo and attacked you, but you defeated those little robots. How? By cutting them up or shooting them? Grenade?"

"Nah. Did some sort of Whispy energy-wave shit." James shrugged. "Don't really know how it worked, just that it did. He's the one who set it up." He grunted and slid to the ground, his back against the wall. "And he's the one who told me what the thing was after we got some good hits on it." He winced a little.

"You okay?"

James nodded. "Yeah, he's put full power to fixing me, or however it works. I hurt a lot less than before, and I don't think I'll even need a healing potion."

"Oh, shit." Shay closed her eyes and took a deep breath.

"What's wrong with me getting better without a healing potion?" James looked up at Shay. "If it's about letting an alien amulet fuck with my body, I think it's way too late to start worrying about that."

"No, that's not what I'm worried about. If anything, we're lucky that you're getting better at using him." Shay shook her head. "You *do* realize the implications of what you fought, don't you, James?"

He shrugged. "Someone sent little robots after me. It was a little annoying to fight the fucker, and he kept changing his attack and getting through my defenses, but Whispy figured something out in the end, so no big deal, right? I just had to let the fucker beat on me first. The Drow got closer to killing me than that thing did." He frowned. "But if I'd had advanced mode then, I probably would have beat their asses easy. Huh. Wonder if I could go to Oriceran and convince them to spar or some shit? Just to kind of measure things."

Shay threw her head back and groaned. "You don't get it, James. This is a *huge* fucking deal, probably the biggest deal since we figured out you were an alien."

"Why?"

"First you have to understand what you fought. We've got nanotechnology on Earth, but that's nothing more than really fancy chemistry on a small scale. I don't understand it, although I know we can make some neat materials. But actual nanites, as in cooperating microscopic robots? That's not something we can do." She scrubbed a hand over her face. "You sure it wasn't magic? Our lives would be much easier if it was magic."

James nodded. "Whispy can tell the difference, and he's adapted to Oriceran magic, Earth magic, and whatever the fuck He Who Hunts' magic was. He's pretty sure it's not magic."

"I had a visitor when you were out," Shay explained after taking a deep breath. "Thought it was a ghost at first, but it was some kind of projected three-dimensional hologram of a woman. Maybe it was magical, but now I'm thinking it wasn't."

"A visitor? Who the fuck was she?"

"Now *that* is the big question." Shay scratched her cheek. "It was some woman who kept going on and on about how you're a monster and you need to be destroyed. She knew about your armor, and I think she knows it's not just an Oriceran artifact. Even though she didn't call you an alien directly, that was what she was getting at. I think the mercenaries and Customs stuff were related to her somehow. I told her to fuck off and tried to stab her, and she disappeared. I think the whole point was to convince me to leave you here to die while the Wendigo did its thing."

James furrowed his brow. "Seriously?"

"Yeah." Shay crossed her arms. "I figured she was a government bitch working with something like Project Ragnarok. That's one of the big reasons I haven't wanted to push deeper into your background, in addition to not believing we can make much progress. Don't want to tip off the government fuckers and give them a new reason to come at you. Only so much Senator Johnston can do."

James grunted.

Shay shook her head. "The problem with this new information is that some things don't make sense. If the woman was with Ragnarok or another government program, American or otherwise, that might explain the advanced technology, like the hologram. But if you were fighting some sort of robot swarm taking the form of a Wendigo… Shit, shit, shit. We *so* didn't need this."

"What the fuck are you talking about?" James asked.

"So, what, the government knows what I am?" He rubbed the back of his neck. "Maybe you're wrong and Senator Johnston can help, even with the secret government programs. He's involved in a lot of black ops shit."

"No, that's just it. He won't be able to help." Shay walked over and squatted in front of James. "Listen to what I'm saying. Even if the government has reverse-engineered alien tech, there's no way in hell they have programmable microrobot swarms with the power to form Wendigos and hurt you. That's not just a few decades in the future, that's like hundreds of years in the future."

James stared at Shay. "Maybe my head's still fucked up from fighting that thing, but I'm not following you. What do you mean it's hundreds of years in the future? They're using magic, then?"

"No. I wish that were the case, but you just told me that Whispy says it's not magic. If it's not magic, it's technology—very advanced technology." Shay dropped to her knees. "Someone's targeting you. Someone who can fuck around on the internet with world-class hacker ease, judging by what Heather told us. Someone who knows what you are, and even knows about your amulet and its ability to adapt to attacks. Someone with advanced technology centuries beyond what we have on Earth." She stared at him. "Do you understand what I'm saying now?"

He winced. "Oh shit. That's…"

"Complicated?"

"Fuck, yeah," James responded. "The Drow were bad enough, but at least I kind of understand how an elf thinks."

Shay sighed. "Exactly. All the evidence points to my

little visitor being some sort of alien too. Not just an alien, but an alien watching your moves close enough to send her nanite assassin after you. The only thing I don't get is why now?"

James furrowed his brow. "The amusement park?"

"Huh?"

He sighed and shrugged. "The fight was out in the open. It had to have been recorded, even if the government suppressed a lot of the stuff. I spent years hiding the amulet, or only using it when it was absolutely necessary. After Maria and her guys saw me in advanced mode and just chalked it up to being a fancy artifact, I stopped worrying so much. I kind of figured anyone from Earth or Oriceran who saw it would assume it was a magical artifact."

"You're right about that." Shay laughed.

"What's so funny?" James frowned.

She shrugged. "Don't you get it? I thought I was being so open-minded and smart by figuring out and accepting you were an alien. All that time it was almost like a game to me. When I found alien artifacts, I thought of them the way I thought of other ancient artifacts, but I'd already found the evidence that pointed to other aliens already being here. Shit. We should have been thinking about it all the time. If there's one non-Oriceran alien, there could be hundreds. Thousands. Fuck, *millions,* for all we know. It's a big universe." She threw up her arms. "Fuck our luck."

"It's not a big deal."

Shay blinked. "How is it not a big deal?"

James grunted. "So someone wants to kill me. How is that new? Them not being from Earth or Oriceran doesn't make it worse. They use fancier tech, but it's all just the same deal: someone tries to fuck me up because they don't like me."

"You're seriously not worried about some alien bitch with advanced technology?" Shay eyed him. "You sure the nanites didn't get in your brain?"

James shrugged. "What's alien even mean anymore? I'm pretty sure He Who Hunts wasn't from Oriceran or Earth. Besides, this might be a good thing."

Shay stared at him. "*A good thing*? How the fuck is some alien bitch hunting you a good thing?"

"If she's following me close enough to send that thing here, then she knows shit like where I'm from." James snorted. "And she's not coming at me personally. If she's an alien, she's probably keeping a low profile, which means she's not gonna blow up LA to get to me, and that makes this not as fucked-up as the shit with He Who Hunts. We can control her; pick our time and place for a battle. Maybe we arm up and go to the middle of the desert and wait for her to send more nanites." He grinned. "I've already adapted to two of her special attacks."

"Okay, I see where you're coming from." Shay nodded. "Still not sold on this being a good thing. Trust me, as a former professional killer, I know that a little patience goes a long way toward taking down a target."

"It's not just that. Whispy knows more than he's telling me. Not sure if he's purposely holding back or if he can't tell me because that's the way he was made or born." James shrugged. "If this alien woman knows the truth about me, maybe we can get it out of her. The more times she comes at me, the more clues we'll have to track her ass down."

"You should understand this isn't your usual pissy-criminal-trying-to-prove-how-badass-she-is situation." Shay shook her head. "You should have heard her. She really thinks you're a bad dude. A monster. To her, I think this is like some sort of holy crusade."

James grunted. "Lots of people think I'm a monster on Earth, and probably Oriceran. Used to it. Fuck, maybe they're even right, but I still don't care."

Shay laughed. "I'm glad someone can be blasé about this shit, because I'm worried."

"You're always worried."

She rolled her eyes. "I'm not always worried."

He shrugged. "Okay, you're worried most of the time. Doesn't matter. Now we know. She took her best shot to take me out, and she blew it. If she's smart, she'll stay hidden in her little alien bunker or spaceship." James stood and shook out his arms. "Fucking Whispy. He's helping me regenerate, but he's not keeping my temperature up. It's cold as a witch's tit here."

"Cold as a witch's tit?" Shay chuckled. "Since when do you say that?"

"Something Trey said. I liked it."

"You would." Shay tilted her head and listened for a moment. "Hear that?"

"What?" James frowned and looked at the door. "I don't hear anything."

"Exactly." Shay headed toward the door and opened it.

Light snow continued to float to the ground, but the harsh winds were gone. There was even a break in the clouds, with a few wonderful rays of warm sunlight coming through.

Shay stepped outside and smiled. "Huh. Wonder if this is just a lull in the storm or if we got lucky."

James followed her, staring at the sky. "Might have had something to do with the Brotherhood or the alien hunting me."

Shay shivered, and not from the cold. "If she can control the weather, we're fucked."

"Nah, just bundle up." James grinned.

His phone rang, and he pulled it out of his pocket with a faint grin. "The sat phones work once we got outside again? So it wasn't an EMP. Killing the head of the Brotherhood did the trick. Or maybe killing the Wendigo did. Didn't think to check after the fights."

Shay shrugged. "The alien bitch made it sound like she was having trouble, too." She pointed to his phone. "Answer it, already."

James tapped to answer the call and activated the speakerphone. "Hey, Heather. We're still alive, and we've killed everyone. There's a break in the blizzard, too. Even the clouds are fucking scared of me today."

Heather laughed. "I'm relieved to hear your voice. I suppose we shouldn't have worried. No way Shay Carson and James Brownstone would be taken out by a cult."

"Also killed a Wendigo, kind of."

Heather didn't respond for several seconds. "Wendigo? As in an abominable snowman?"

"Like I said, kind of." James grunted.

Heather sighed. "Okay, then. Anyway, we've got some stuff to talk to you about, including someone poking around. Someone damned good. We've been trying to trace them back so we can counter-hack, but this might be a problem in the future, and I'm going to be upfront. We still have no clue who it might be."

"Shay and I have a good idea who it is," James replied. "Kind of."

"What the hell?" Heather replied. "You knew about this already? Why didn't you tell us someone was going to be hacking around looking for you?"

"We didn't know about it before. We figured it out on this job."

Heather groaned. "You're confusing the hell out of me, James. What happened up there? I thought you were just killing some cultists and grabbing a magical urn."

James looked at Shay. "It's a long story. I think I'll wait until we're back in America to go through it. Short version is someone new wants to kill me, and they've got access to special toys to do it."

Heather chuckled. "Isn't that your normal, everyday life?"

He smirked. "Yeah, it is. We'll wait to make sure the storm is clearing out and contact the Canadian government. You guys don't have to worry about active support. We're good here."

"Okay, then. See you soon."

James smiled. "Yeah. Can't wait to get back to palm trees and fucking sunshine."

# CHAPTER TWENTY-ONE

Kathy eyed the two huge palm trees in front of the empty black two-story commercial building. "Those are kind of cool, but I feel like if they fall for any reason, we're going to have a very expensive repair on our hands and a lot of dead customers. Already going to need to renovate it to turn it into a bar as it is." She rubbed her chin. "Just don't know."

Tyler laughed. "This is Vegas, Kathy. It's not like they get hurricanes. It's also not like the trees will fall over the minute we buy the building."

"They get nasty thunder and wind storms here." Kathy shrugged. "And excuse me for wanting to be careful, considering I'm putting my money into this project. I figured a miser like you would want to be careful, too."

"I'm not a miser. I'm a careful businessman who likes to minimize expenses." Tyler crossed his arms and shook his head. "While we're bitching about stuff, I'm still not sold on the name."

Kathy smiled. "White Sun is cooler than Black Sun or

Black Sun II. You want to be related but not suggest a simple copy." She shook a finger. "Trust me on this."

"Maybe." Tyler sighed. "So much for my branding."

She rolled her eyes. "It's not like you were going to be able to franchise to a hundred cities or something. Your business model is only so scalable. You're going to have to let go a little if you want to make more money. There's only so much a single individual can do and control."

"Maria said something similar." Tyler shook his head, then chuckled. "White Sun…whatever. You're putting up enough money that you should have some say."

Kathy pivoted on the sidewalk and watched as cars flowed by. "Good access to the road, decent parking. Pretty close to the Strip. Not sure if that's a good thing or a bad thing, but at least it's something. We'll have to see what the other sites look like." A coy smile took over her face. "It's still weird to think about."

"What is?" Tyler frowned.

She gestured to the building. "All this. It wasn't all that long ago I was moving to LA from New York, and now I'm moving again."

Tyler shrugged. "It wasn't all that long ago that the Black Sun was a shitty hole in the wall. Times change."

Kathy blinked.

He frowned. "What?"

"Nothing. Just weird to see you drop the cocky front."

Tyler snorted. "Says the woman who was acting all tough and then OCD'd over some mysteries. We all have our masks, and they slip sometimes. If I'm going into business with you, there's only so much I can bullshit you."

"True enough." Kathy frowned. "Speaking of mysteries, I wonder if this means I can get out of it?"

Tyler turned away from the building toward her. "Get out of what?"

"Owing the Eyes an answer." She shrugged. "Whatever the hell that means. One good thing about getting out of LA is that I'll have to deal with him a lot less, if at all. Just the thought of him still makes my skin crawl."

"Doubt it." Tyler shook his head. "Whatever the hell he is, I don't think he's the kind of creature who'll just forget that someone owes him something. Not that I blame you for wanting to stay away from him. I fucking *hate* talking to him." He gave her a dark grin. "But if you're going to make anything of the White Sun, you'll have to connect with a whole new set of freaks here." He pointed at the street as a red Lexus sped past. "Vegas might not be as big as LA, but it's just as crazy, if not crazier, in its own way. I've heard they've got an actual mermaid who lives in the Golden Nugget's shark tank."

"Sounds kind of cool, but I get your point." Kathy nodded. "I know. And I also get that there's no real way to run from your past."

"Fuck the past. Worry about the future. You secure your future, it doesn't matter if your past catches up with you. And keep in mind, just like with LA, Brownstone's always got people here. At this very moment, he's got Trey and some men here." Tyler turned back toward the building. "The Brownstone Agency will be the key to this. We'll have to get them backing our place for it to work, and if the Eyes makes a stink, they'll be the key to getting him to back off."

"Are you sure that'll even work? It's not that I don't like the idea of having the Brownstone Agency backing me, but it's not as simple as throwing money at them. They may be bounty hunters, but they're about more than just money."

"Yeah, sure. That makes this even easier because we can get their help without having to throw a lot of money at them, if any."

Kathy's face scrunched in confusion. "How do you figure?"

"By understanding their psychology." Tyler chuckled darkly. "Do you know what Trey's doing right now?"

"Hunting bounties." Kathy shrugged. "That's what he does on most days he's working."

"No, he's not hunting bounties."

"What?" She frowned. "He's on vacation, then, hitting shows and casinos?"

Tyler shook his head. "You see, bounty hunting is what he normally does, but he's got a more important job right now."

"A more important job than bounty hunting?"

"Brownstone's got a favorite barbeque place here. From what I hear, it's his favorite barbeque place in the whole damned country, a place called Jessie Rae's. Supposed to be one of the best places in the country for that kind of thing." Tyler shrugged. "Don't know. I'm not a barbeque aficionado."

Kathy nodded. "I've heard him mention it. What about it? Is Trey doing something with Jessie Rae's for Brownstone's barbeque team or something?" She chuckled. "Talk about me being OCD, but I've got nothing on that guy and his barbeque obsession."

Tyler shrugged. "Place got robbed, so Trey's ripping up Vegas looking for the guy who did it. Really hitting the town." He turned back to the building and narrowed his eyes. "Think about that. Trey could be helping the other guys pick up bounties, making himself piles of money, but instead he's been spending money and time looking for someone who robbed a barbeque joint with all the effort he might put into a level-four bounty.

"It's not like Jessie Rae's pays Brownstone anything. From what I've heard, they give his people a discount, not even free food, but now someone's going to go down hard because they offended Brownstone and his people. If they had robbed any other barbeque joint in town, they would have had only to worry about the overworked police, but now Trey's coming for them. And if Trey doesn't find them, Brownstone will come like some sort of Angel of Vengeance, and not because of the money. Not because of justice, but because of something personal—barbeque."

Kathy burst out laughing.

Tyler frowned. "What's so funny?"

She calmed the laughing down to quiet chuckles. "So the only thing we need to do to get Brownstone's help is produce the best barbeque in the country?"

Tyler shrugged. "I'm sure we don't have to go that far. The point is, we can get the agency's help if we give them a personal reason to give a shit. I'm sure that between the two of us, we can come up with something."

"I'm not going to bang somebody in the agency just for protection," Kathy replied.

Tyler frowned. "That's not why the AET started protecting my place."

Kathy smirked. "Just a fringe benefit?" She nodded toward his car. "Let's go check out the next place and worry about the Brownstone Agency later."

---

James held the door as Heather rolled her wheelchair into the conference room at Camp Brownstone. Shay and Peyton already sat at the long conference table, pensive looks on their faces.

Heather continued toward the table and nodded to the others.

*Wonder why James was so mysterious on the phone? I get that he didn't want to talk about it in the middle of Alberta, but even once he got back to Calgary, he didn't want to explain anything. What the hell happened up there?*

Shay looked at James. "Sure you want to do this here? We could do it at a warehouse."

He shrugged and walked over to the table to take a seat. "Here's fine. Just didn't want to do this online, especially since we're not sure if our mystery hacker can easily spy on us. Considering all the shit that went down, I'm guessing the more we stick to our places in LA, the less chance she has of poking at me."

Peyton frowned. "Heather and I are working on countermeasures for the online stuff. Yeah, it annoys me to admit it, but maybe it doesn't hurt to go old-school at times." He shot Shay a glance. "And it's nice to get out of the warehouse now and then."

Shay smirked.

James grunted. "I'm sure you guys will come up with something."

Heather shrugged. "It might help if we knew who is behind everything. The phone you picked up was connected to a regular old-fashioned dirtbag mercenary outfit. I managed to dig into their finances, and they did get a huge payment recently, but whoever paid them did a good job of burying their trail a number of ways, including using several different crypto-wallets. From what you said on the phone, it seems like you have some idea who is behind all this."

An uncomfortable expression appeared on Peyton's face. He looked at Shay and James.

Heather frowned. "Why do I get the feeling you three already know the answer, and I'm the only clueless one here?"

"First, there's something important you need to know about me," James rumbled. "Everything kind of relates to that."

"Okay. What?"

"I'm an alien," James rumbled.

Heather blinked. "Excuse me?"

"An alien," he repeated with a shrug. "You know, like an extraterrestrial. I wasn't born on Earth. I was born on another planet."

"You're Oriceran?" Heather nodded slowly. "I guess certain things make more sense now. You're too tough to be a normal human, even without your amulet artifact. I always kind of figured, but I hacked your DNA records, and they looked human enough. You use magic to fake test results or something? Or wait, are you saying you're a human born on Oriceran?"

James grunted. "Surprised with all the digging around you've done on me you didn't already figure some of this out, but you're still not getting it."

Heather shrugged. "Then enlighten me, James."

Shay and Peyton sighed.

James shook his head. "I'm not Oriceran. I mean, I'm not human, but I'm also not from Oriceran. I was born on a different planet. Turns out there are other planets with intelligent beings, not just Oriceran and Earth. I didn't know this for most of my life, but now I do. Other people do too, including people in the government, but they're keeping it secret."

Heather laughed. "Okay, good one, James. You being Mr. Stoic makes it easy for you to deliver lines like that straight-faced. For a second, just a second, I started to believe you before realizing how ridiculous this all sounds."

She looked at Shay and Peyton. Neither was laughing.

*Oh, shit. No way.*

"It's not a joke," James rumbled. "I'm telling you all this because Shay had contact during the Alberta job with some sort of hologram of a woman who we think is also an alien, and who has it in for me for some reason. Maybe something from my home planet." He shrugged. "I don't know shit about my home planet, so that complicates things. For all I know, this is some sort of blood feud over shit my ancestors did five hundred years ago or something. Who the fuck knows?"

Heather stared at him for a long while before allowing herself to speak, her mind straining to push past the Earth-

Oriceran dichotomy. "Okay, if it was another alien, and I can't believe I'm saying those words, that might explain why there was so much strangeness with the hacking attacks Peyton and I were dealing with. They felt different than when I've run into magic hacking." She frowned. "Wait, so everyone already knew about this but me?"

Peyton gave her an apologetic look and shrugged.

Shay grinned. "I'm the one who figured it out. I knew before James did. I needed Peyton's help at the time, so I dragged him into it."

James grunted and patted his chest. "Don't feel too bad. *I* didn't even know for most of my life. The amulet I use isn't magic, it's alien technology. I've had it since I was a kid; I was found with it when I was little. It's intelligent, and speaks to me in my mind. I used to not be able to understand, but I understand it more and more now. I think that's connected with me being able to use more of its ability."

Heather rubbed her temples. "Now things are just getting weird. So, you're saying you're an alien wearing an alien?"

He shook his head. "I don't think it's a lifeform. I think it's technology; a device with a mind in it."

"Biological artificial intelligence?" Heather pinched the bridge of her nose. "This gets more complicated with each thing you explain."

James snorted. "Think about how *I* feel. I don't understand everything about it, but, yeah, the way it talks in my mind, it's almost like a computer. I think even though it's alive, it's something my people made. I don't think it can live by itself."

"A symbiont?"

He frowned. "I guess you could call it that. I've always just thought of it as 'the amulet,' but Shay gave it a nickname, and now I call it that."

Heather glanced at Shay. "And what's the nickname?"

"Whispy Doom," Shay responded. "It's a very bloodthirsty little amulet, so I was joking about how it's always whispering doom ideas."

James frowned.

"Of course." Heather snickered. "Advanced biotechnology. Living computers." Heather nodded. "Even though scientists are doing that kind of research here, the average elf might not live long enough to see humans produce something like that."

James grunted. "Yeah, the damned thing won't give me useful answers that don't have to do with kicking ass, so we have to figure out how to deal with this shit ourselves." He frowned down at the amulet covered by his shirt. "Even though I need the little bastard to protect myself, like from the Wendigo that turned out to be a bunch of nanites."

"Nanites too?" Heather whistled. "Don't know if I should be scared or impressed."

Shay shrugged. "So now you're in on the big secret, Heather. Based on what James fought in Alberta and what I was told, this alien bitch is trying to keep a low profile, which is something we can use to our advantage."

Peyton nodded. "Makes sense to me. Even if she really has it in for James' species, it's not like humans will care about that, and the government's not going to like any advanced technology they don't control. Most of the alien-hunting projects we've come across don't seem all that friendly."

James leaned back and nodded.

"That's one thing that does worry me," Shay added. "The technology displayed in Canada was centuries ahead of what we have on Earth. If this bitch is sniffing around via the internet, I don't know if we can beat her without special magic or something, and the more people we bring in, the greater the risk."

Heather shook her head. "Not necessarily."

The other three looked her way.

"You know someone?" Shay asked.

"No. That's not what I was getting at. Being super-advanced in technology isn't necessarily a huge advantage." Heather pulled out her phone and brought up a picture of a rotary telephone. She set the phone on the table and spun it to face the others. "Hacking's not just about having the best technology, it's about understanding and taking advantage of the information technology infrastructure. There are inherent limits to that, because you're somewhat limited by that same existing information technology infrastructure regardless of how smart you are."

Peyton's eyes widened. "Of course. I never thought of it that way."

James frowned and looked at Shay.

She shrugged and glanced at Peyton and Heather. "Not following. Don't think he is, either."

"Say I got transported back to the mid-1800s," Heather explained. "My advanced knowledge would help me with stuff like the telegraph, but it's not like my knowledge of programming or modern networking technology would mean I could suddenly do magic with telegraph wires. I can only exploit the network to the limits of capability. Phone phreaks could get free calls, but they couldn't call the moon." She shrugged. "The tech inherently limits some of the possibilities."

Peyton nodded. "So even with her fancy alien gadgets, we might not be totally outclassed, just *mostly* outclassed."

"All we need is a chance," Shay replied. "We get James in the room with this bitch and he and Whispy can send her running all the way back to whatever fucking planet she comes from."

Heather frowned. "Even though this all sounds insane on one level, for some reason I want to believe it. But that leads me to the next obvious question: if some weird alien is hunting James, why not just call the government and ask for their help? From what you said, they're already out there looking for bad aliens."

Shay frowned. "The short version is that even though there are government forces who are tracking aliens, they're dangerous, so we've been careful to keep any information suggesting James is an alien away from the government. If we get lucky, maybe they'll key into this alien bitch if she overreaches and take her out. But if we lead them to James, they'll probably lock him up in some weird lab. We can't take the risk. He can take on an alien hunting him, but he can't win against the entire government."

Heather sighed. "We're supposed to fight this mysterious advanced alien by ourselves?"

Shay shrugged and grinned. "We've been dealing with government conspiracies by ourselves, so why not add a hostile alien or two? And to be clear, the only people who know about this are in this room. Trey, Maria, and Royce—none of them know."

Heather took a deep breath. "I don't know if I should be honored or scared."

James nodded. "The bottom line is, I don't care if alien fuckers want to come at me. Humans have. Oricerans have. Other shit has. The more the fucking merrier. Someday I'll finally kick enough ass that these fuckers will understand they do *not* come at me."

"Don't ever change, James." Shay laughed.

He looked around the table. "But one thing I've been forced to learn is that I can't do this shit all by myself. I need people to have my back. Just because the alien fucked up this time doesn't mean she'll give up." He locked eyes with Heather. "But you also have a kid, and I'm not gonna drag you into my bullshit. When you signed up with me, you didn't know about any of this alien shit, so if you want to walk away, it's fine by me. I'll even help you relocate if you want since I'm the one who encouraged you to move here."

Heather looked down and sighed. She shook her head. "No. You gave me my life back, and a future. Besides, I don't like the idea of this alien thinking she can walk all over me on the internet. This is *my* planet, not hers." She looked up with a smile. "And if I can keep counter-hacking some alien who thinks I'm just a dumb ape, I'll have hacker cred to the day I die when I can finally talk about this. Don't worry, James, I've got your back."

Peyton grinned and rubbed his hands. "This is going to be fun."

Shay eyed him. "Yeah, except for all the nanite-monster assassins."

"Well, they aren't coming after me." He shrugged. "It won't be fun for James, but it'll be fun for me."

Heather snorted.

*Still can't decide if signing up with James was the best thing I've ever done or the stupidest, but whatever it is, no one can call it boring.*

James stood. "Thanks, Heather. I appreciate it. Didn't want to just drop all this on you and run, but I've got to head to Vegas. Trey scored a location on where the Jessie Rae's thief has been hiding."

Heather nodded. "Surprised with everything you've gone through that's still on your priority list."

"Top of the fucking list." He shrugged. "Probably lots of aliens who want to kill me, but there's only one Jessie Rae's."

# CHAPTER TWENTY-TWO

Trey smiled as he leaned against the railing at the top of the stairwell. He cracked his knuckles and reached into his pockets to pull out Zoe's gloves. After slipping them on, he nodded to his fellow bounty hunters down the stairs. They nodded back and strolled to the side of the building. He returned his attention to the apartment door.

*Here's the home of the dumbest motherfucker on the planet. Well, maybe I should be fair. He might not have known who would be pissed about him robbing Jessie Rae's, so he might just be the* unluckiest *motherfucker on the planet.*

"Nah," Trey murmured. "Definitely the dumbest."

He pushed off the railing and strolled toward the apartment door. Even though he wanted to deliver a classic LA beat-down, the target didn't have a bounty, so he would need to be careful to avoid assault charges. He needed to make it self-defense.

*This shit's gonna be fun. I'm usually trying to talk assholes down, not hyping a fight, but it don't matter as long as I get the trophies back and he ends up in jail.*

Trey stopped in front of the door and adjusted his tie. "Time to see how smart Demetrius is." He rapped the door and plastered a pleasant smile on his face as he waited.

A half-minute passed before the door creaked open, a single dark eye staring out through the crack. "Who the fuck are you? I don't need religion."

"Oh, you need far more than that," Trey responded. "Hey, Demetrius, can we chat?"

"I don't know you, asshole. How do you know my name? You best get the fuck out of here before I throw your ass over the railing."

*Keep going, motherfucker. Give me a reason.*

Trey chuckled. "But you've built up such a reputation lately, Demetrius. I bet everybody in Vegas knows who you are now."

The door opened wider to reveal the man's unimpressive wardrobe choices of a wifebeater, jeans, and a gold chain. His face matched the security camera images exactly. Either he had robbed Jessie Rae's, or someone was using magic to look exactly like some random sonofabitch from Huntridge.

Trey nodded. "Yeah, you don't know me, but I know you, and we've got to chat a little about your recent activities. I'm hoping it can be pleasant, but that's on you."

Demetrius sneered. "Oh, you're that Brownstone bitch who's been asking around about me." He snorted. "I'll give you credit. You managed to find me here, but you're gonna regret that shit, bitch."

"You can call me Trey Garfield," Trey responded. "Neither my first, middle, nor last name is 'Bitch.'"

"I ain't got no bounty, bounty hunter." Demetrius smirked. "If you come at me, you're just a thug, and the police are gonna haul your ass off."

"The police might want to talk to you too," Trey replied. "And even if you don't have a bounty, you robbed Jessie Rae's, so you're my problem and the big man's problem."

"Big man?"

"James Brownstone, motherfucker." Trey offered Demetrius his own sneer and scratched his cheek. "We can do this a couple of ways. One way is you hand over any shit you still have from Jessie Rae's, and I march you down to the police station, where you turn yourself in. The other way is you try some dumb shit and I beat your ass down, and then I drag you down to the police station anyway. You see, we've got you on the security camera, and I'm sure your dumb ass left fingerprints and DNA, too."

Demetrius' face twitched. "Bullshit. That's impossible. You don't have me on no security camera. You're lying, bitch."

Trey laughed. "What, you thought your little magic knife saved you? That's the problem with playing with new toys without manuals. Don't always understand them." His smile vanished, and he glared at the other man. "Now, I'm gonna be honest. I'd love it if you chose option number two, because then I get to beat your ass down in self-defense, and I'll help you understand why you don't fuck with Jessie Rae's. What's it gonna be, Demetrius? Number one or number two?"

Demetrius looked Trey up and down before nodding.

"Fine, fuck it. I don't want no trouble. It ain't worth it over some barbeque joint." He shrugged. "Let me at least get my coat."

Trey arched a brow. "You expect me to believe that shit? Turn around and put your hands on your head. I'm gonna cuff your ass, then we're gonna walk down the stairs to the fine Expedition I have parked and drive you to the nearest fucking police station. I'm guessing Jessie Rae's ain't the only place you've robbed lately."

They locked eyes, both barely taking a breath. The seconds ticked by, each waiting for the other's move.

Demetrius spun on his heel and sprinted off. He hurdled over the couch and rushed into the bedroom.

"Thank you, Demetrius," Trey murmured. "I almost thought you would give up and the fun would be over."

As pissed as Trey was, he couldn't bring himself to beat down a man who had willingly surrendered.

He didn't follow the thief. He snorted and waited. If Demetrius were trying to flee, his only option would be to jump from the balcony outside his bedroom. The other bounty hunters were watching the balcony, and they were ready to stun Demetrius' thieving ass.

The safest way out would be through one man—Trey—and the front door.

*Come on, bitch. You don't want to run. Show me how tough you are. Stand and fight. Give me a fucking excuse.*

A few seconds later, Demetrius stepped out of his bedroom, a thin bone knife in his hand and a wide grin on his face.

"Now we're talking." Trey nodded. "Good, you didn't

try to run away. That makes this shit less annoying, and a lot more fun for me."

Demetrius raised the knife. "You think you're tough, bounty bitch? This shit is magic. You ain't have no idea what you're fucking with."

"Yeah, because I ain't ever seen any magic in my job?" Trey snorted. "Bitch, please. My girlfriend is a witch, and I work with a witch. I've taken down level fours. You think whatever weak-ass magic knife you've got is gonna scare me? I should beat your ass down for being a stupid motherfucker."

The criminal pointed the knife and glared at Trey. "Fuck you. You're dead, bitch." He shouted a word in a language Trey didn't understand.

Flames swirled around the tip of the knife, but the slow charge allowed Trey to leap to the side before the flames condensed into a bright fireball and blasted his way. The ball smashed into the railing behind him, punching through and splattering molten metal all over the place. A stray drop burned through Trey's jacket before landing with a sizzle on the ground.

"Oh, *hell* no," he shouted and hopped to his feet. "It's bad enough you fuck with Jessie Rae's, but now you've done fucked up my suit, Demetrius. You've gone and made this personal."

Trey rushed into the apartment. Demetrius shouted the incantation again, but the bounty hunter smashed a gloved fist into his face while the weapon was still charging. The knife flew out of the criminal's hand, and the flames vanished.

Demetrius grunted and flew backward. He crashed into

his brown entertainment center, the wood splintering and his speakers smacking into the wall. His falling leg caught a power cord, yanking his TV off the wall. The flat panel fell and struck a hard corner of the entertainment center, impaling the device.

Trey snatched the knife off the floor and shook his head. "Damn. After you get out of jail, you'll have to replace all that shit. So now you're all beat up, and your shit's messed up. Not your lucky day, Demetrius."

The criminal groaned.

Trey held up the knife. "And a bonus. You see, I had some people I know check around once I heard you had a magic knife. I was wondering if one had gone missing, and damned if they quickly found out which one was missing. So, this is great because you're going to jail, and even though there's no bounty on you, I'm gonna score some cash from returning this knife." He tapped the side of his head with the hilt of the weapon. "You're such a petty piece of shit, Demetrius. You manage to get yourself something like this, and you're using it to rob restaurants?"

Demetrius groaned and managed to stand. Blood trailed down the side of his head. "Fuck you. You don't know nothing about me, Mr. Slick Suit. I do what I do because I need to survive," he yelled and charged Trey.

The bounty hunter didn't bother to dodge, just slammed a fist into the criminal's stomach. Demetrius' eyes bulged, and he fell to the ground clutching his belly.

Trey snorted. "You're lucky I'm holding back, and don't feed me that excuses shit. We all make choices. You can sit there and cry about how society fucked you over or your mama or whoever else the fuck you want to cry about, but you're the one choosing in the end. No one held a gun to your head and told you to rob a barbeque place."

Demetrius moaned and rolled to his side, still clutching himself.

Trey shook his head. "I used to be a piece of shit too, and I ain't got no good excuse. I had Nana telling me I was a piece of shit, but I ignored her. I realize all that now. I like to say that I needed a new opportunity, but I could have chosen not to be trash long before that. I didn't need James Brownstone to save me, even though he did. That's the real tragedy. I could have saved my own ass from the beginning." He tossed the knife on the couch and knelt by the groaning Demetrius. "Let me deliver a few words from a wise man who died a long time ago and had more power than either of us will ever know. '*You* have power over your mind, not outside events. Realize this, and you will find strength.'"

"Fuck you," Demetrius rasped. He spat in Trey's face. "I'll fucking gut you, bounty hunter. This shit ain't over. You think you're tough? You ain't nothing."

"Some people just have closed minds." Trey sighed and shook his head.

"Problem?" rumbled a deep voice from behind Trey. "It's taking a while. I thought you'd already have him in the Expedition, or the other guys would have gotten him."

Trey turned around and grinned at James. "Sorry, I was trying to provide a free education to this dumb motherfucker, but he's proving...stubborn."

James looked around, his gaze focusing on the knife before drifting to the broken entertainment center and dented wall. He grunted and nodded. "I see."

Demetrius' eyes widened. "James Brownstone."

Trey nodded. "Yeah. He was busy when I started looking for you. He ain't busy now. He was waiting downstairs for us." He shrugged. "I've got one question for you, Demetrius. The plaques and trophies you took from Jessie Rae's. I know you didn't move that shit yet. Where the fuck are they? If you don't want to tell me, then you can have a chat with the big man. I have to let you know, he's nowhere near as nice as me."

"B-b-bedroom closet," Demetrius stammered and swallowed. A dark stain appeared at his crotch.

"Yeah, you're so tough." Trey laughed and stood, shaking out his hands. "I'll go get the shit, James. You keep an eye on King Pisser here. Maybe I should have one of the boys go buy him a diaper."

James stomped to the fallen Demetrius, a feral grin on his face. "Go ahead and do something. Prove what a tough asshole you are."

The thief's eyes rolled up in the back of his head, and he passed out.

Trey snorted as he headed into the bedroom. "What a weak-ass bitch."

He threw open the closet. A large black trash bag sat inside. Various trophies and plaques from Jessie Rae's were in it, along with jewelry and some cash.

"Looks like our boy's been busy," Trey shouted to the living room. "Not just Jessie Rae's. But I've got Mike's stuff in here."

"Good," James replied, his voice low and filled with dangerous promise. "Too bad he didn't put up more of a fight."

Trey grabbed the loot bag and hauled it into the living room. He pulled out his phone and snapped a few pictures of the urine-soaked and unconscious criminal. "Should get Heather to plaster this shit everywhere with some funny title."

James chuckled. "Good idea."

# CHAPTER TWENTY-THREE

Aiyn paced in front of her ocean-view window, her breathing shallow. A failure. A complete failure. Worse than that, the attacks had wounded Brownstone but hadn't finished him, which meant his symbiont was stronger—and she'd lost two good attack methods that could harm the Forerunner. She'd made the monster stronger.

She moved over to her chaise lounge and sat down, sighing.

*I should have won. If the magical spells hadn't disrupted my initial connection to the nanoform, I could have directed it more effectively, and it wouldn't have relied on the base programming. Or was it a mistake to use my limited communications to try to convince Carson of Brownstone's danger? I thought she was being deceived, but I should have stuck to the initial plan where a mysterious local monster killed everyone and the Canadian government was none the wiser about my involvement.*

Aiyn frowned. The easiest solution would have been to bomb the area, but that would have been difficult to justify to her superiors, given that they didn't want her to attack Brownstone. As it was, careful auditing of her supply reports might reveal the depletion of her nanite stock and result in her recall.

For a moment, she considered purposely admitting to the attack. If they sent a replacement, maybe her superiors would be more inclined to consider the Forerunner threat real, but she couldn't risk them delaying sending someone else. Brownstone might show his true nature at any time. It'd be too late by the time he summoned a Vanguard.

No, it fell to her to solve the problem.

Aiyn sighed. Losing the entire nanoform was a blow. It'd take her months to grow her nanite supply back, and any request for resupply would lead to her recall from Earth. They didn't accept that James Brownstone was a Vax Forerunner.

*No nanites, but I could confront him directly—although if I don't kill him in one shot I'll die, and it might initiate the invasion. I might not have months, not with the power he's openly displaying.*

She frowned. In her arrogance, she'd hoped to goad Shay Carson into leaving Brownstone in Alberta. Aiyn had been convinced he'd die at the hands of her nanoform. The plan had seemed perfect when she'd thought of it.

*I was careful not to state what I was, but if he understood what attacked him, he knows he's being hunted by something far more dangerous than a human. He might accelerate his timetable.*

The last few days of government reports didn't suggest any unusual activity she could associate with Brownstone.

Her gambit might have failed, but it hadn't initiated the next stage of the invasion. She still had time to save Earth.

She revisited the idea of trying to involve Earth authorities, given that Brownstone hadn't reacted in the way she'd worried he would, but the dangerous Earth groups hunting aliens might care less about her warnings and more about capturing her and taking her technology. The Concealment Protocol had been born of dangerous failures by past Shepherds. Even if she didn't mind giving her life to defeat the Vax, she didn't want to give it mindlessly. Her recent failure had driven home that careful plans could amount to nothing when the enemy behaved outside the expected parameters.

Whatever she did next, she had to plan not only the operation but also how to protect Earth should she die. She couldn't depend on the Alliance, even if they should know better.

*There has to be another possibility. A better possibility.*

Aiyn thought back to her conversation with Shay Carson. The tomb raider's words suggested she understood Brownstone's true nature. The Shepherd had never thought there could be a Vax collaborator, but the unique situation between Earth and Oriceran might have produced something unexpected.

*I'm beginning to see the wisdom in Command not wanting me to confront him directly. Something's wrong and different, even more than I realized. If I'm to defeat Brownstone before he summons the Vanguard, I need to understand his new tactics and why he's spent so many years studying Earth.*

Aiyn allowed herself a small smile. Even though her recent attempts at digging more into Shay Carson's background had been thwarted by unexpected resistance, her previous efforts had recovered several useful pieces of information, including the fact the tomb raider lectured as a professor at UCLA. That little tidbit presented an opportunity. If she were cautious, she could get close to Carson, and through her, Brownstone.

If a Vax Forerunner could be subtle, so could Aiyn.

"Time to study history," she murmured.

---

James kept a light hold on Thomas' leash as they headed down the sidewalk, Shay at his side. He smiled to himself as he looked around, enjoying the crisp-but-not-freezing air and the lack of anything even approaching snow. The last few days hadn't even threatened rain. A pleasant but not too cool December.

*I bet hell isn't hot. I bet it's cold. Real fucking cold.*

"Alison's return home is getting closer by the day," Shay declared. "You haven't said much about going anywhere. I didn't want to pressure you, but you were the one who originally brought up the idea."

He shook his head. "No fucking way. Sometimes the best way to spend the holidays is by sitting your ass at home. And home is LA. Snow is complicated. The last thing I want to do is make our holidays complicated."

Shay shrugged. "Don't have to go anywhere cold, you know." She smirked.

"Not going anywhere." James grunted.

Thomas barked.

Shay laughed. "Can't blame you, although I have to

admit, I actually *do* feel more relaxed despite all the shit that went down. I guess I really did need to get some of that out of my system."

"Me, too. All the more reason to stay close to home." James shrugged. "Did you know Alison's afraid to bring a boyfriend home? She acts like I'm gonna kill them if they step into my house."

"Can you blame her? Every time she even tries to hint at something, you act like you're going to fly to the school and attempt a field goal with any boy who looks at her." Shay rolled her eyes. "And you look smug and happy about it, too."

James shrugged. "I think I've improved a little."

Shay snorted. "Need a microscope to see that level of improvement. Just saying, if you want her to share all of her life with you, you need to cut down on the implied threats to other people she might care about. Okay?"

"I kind of see where you're coming from."

Thomas barked at a passing car.

Shay smiled at the dog. "Besides, James, Alison's magic has advanced a lot, and we both spent a summer teaching her to kick ass without magic. She's helped you on bounties. If anything, at this point the boys should probably be more afraid of *her* than of you."

James brightened. "You think so?"

She snorted. "Don't be too happy about that. She's growing up, and love and relationships are part of that. Sorry, Daddy, someday you'll have to let your little girl go."

"I guess that's true." James frowned. "Even if it took *me* a long time to get into that sort of thing."

"What sort of thing?" Shay grinned. "Love?"

His face twitched. "Are you gonna give me shit if I admit I still don't understand a lot of this crap?"

Shay shook her head. "Yeah, I get that, because you referring to our relationship as 'this crap' kind of shows you have a longer way to go than you think." She chuckled. "But I also know you still listen to that relationship podcast, so you're trying. That's the important thing, so I try not to bust your balls too much."

James focused on Thomas' wagging tail as they turned a corner. "Been thinking a lot about things lately. Was kind of thinking about it before we went to Canada, and then all that annoying shit happened and distracted me, but now that I'm back here, I've got plenty of time to think."

"For a guy who likes things simple, you sure overthink everything."

He shrugged. "Just saying. Isn't thinking a good thing?"

"Sometimes. If you're thinking the right way about the right kind of thing." Shay nodded. "And what have you been thinking about?"

"The future," James replied.

"The future?" Shay eyed him, suspicion on her face. "What about the future?"

He nodded. "Isn't that what you should think about when you're in a relationship?"

Shay blinked. "That's…one school of thought."

James stared at her. Being with Shay made him feel something he hadn't experienced before he met her. It made him give a shit about living in a way he hadn't before. Maybe that was love, maybe that was something else. For all he knew, his species might not be capable of love.

Whispy Doom seemed far more focused on getting him pissed off than protecting others.

*The future. We could have one together. Alison would like Shay to be her stepmom. Father McCartney would probably stop frowning about me shacking up. Is it right, though? I keep telling myself it's better for Shay to not be married, but she's made her choice, and she keeps picking me.*

*She's smarter than I am. There's no way she hasn't thought through all this shit already. I should stop trying to take the choice from her.*

James cleared his throat. "Shay, about the future…"

Shay put up a hand. "Wait."

"Wait?"

She gave him a curt nod and a mischievous smile. "I'm a woman whose whole life has been nothing but a leaf blowing on the wind. If something big, something permanent, is going to change that, I hope the first step in that would be epic. Not just epic. *Fucking* epic, because then I'd know that the theoretical person who might want to pull the leaf out of the wind understands what they are doing and isn't just trying to make something complicated simple because it's convenient for them." She stared into his eyes. "Do we understand each other, Mr. James Brownstone?"

"Yeah." James grunted. "I'll take that under advisement. 'Fucking epic?'"

Shay nodded. "Fucking *epic*, and that requires planning."

Thomas barked and wagged his tail.

Shay grinned. "While we're on the subject of the future, there are a few fancy restaurants I want to go to while Alison is here."

James stared into the distance as Shay tortured him with various barbeque-free suggestions.

*"Fucking epic?" What do women find fucking epic? What does* Shay *find fucking epic?*

*Damn it. Will the relationship podcast help me figure out the best way to propose to a tomb raider?*

*FINIS*

# AUTHOR NOTES - MICHAEL ANDERLE

## NOVEMBER 15, 2018

THANK YOU for not only reading this story but these *Author Notes* as well .

(I think I've been good with always opening with "thank you." If not, I need to edit the other *Author Notes*!)

RANDOM (*sometimes*) THOUGHTS?

Today I received a question from a fan about the Glorious PITA (from TKG21) but the reader was asking because of *Payback is a Bitch* (TKE01), which made me wonder if the reader had read the first twenty-one books in TKG, or it had just been long enough that she had forgotten the tag for a Kurtherian who had tracked TOM down near Earth. That caused me to question...

Can a series go on too long (even if the stories are good?)

This is, without a doubt, a book-publishing marketing question as well as a more esoteric question on the scope of stories.

I put the caveat about the stories are good to just focus on the number of titles.

I'd be curious as to your thoughts. Feel free to join us on the Oriceran Facebook page to discuss this series, or in the reviews of the series or just wherever you wish to drop a note

HOW TO MARKET FOR BOOKS YOU LOVE

We are able to support our efforts with you reading our books, and we appreciate you doing this!

If you enjoyed this or ANY book by any author, especially Indie-published, we always appreciate if you make the time to review a book, since it lets other readers who might be on the fence to take a chance on it as well.

AROUND THE WORLD IN 80 DAYS

One of the interesting (at least to me) aspects of my life is the ability to work from anywhere and at any time. In the future, I hope to re-read my own *Author Notes* and remember my life as a diary entry.

Dear Mike,

You are sitting in your chair writing at your desk at the Veer. The sun is close to hiding behind the mountains west of Las Vegas, throwing your room into shade (fast!) For some reason, Alexa (Amazon Music) has decided to play American / CW-style music, and I'm finding myself wanting to look out over fields of grain.

Kind of hard to find any fields of grain looking down Las Vegas Blvd South.

Damned country-western music – I'm starting to wave

my head back and forth listening. I don't normally listen to CW music (except *Indian Outlaw* by Tim McGraw…That shit is the bomb. I've no idea how politically correct this song is, but the fiddle and drums and stuff are kickass. Coming from a devout Heavy Metal listener… That's some righteous music, man. His "get this shit done" attitude in the music speaks to me.)

Ok, I had Alexa play *Indian Outlaw*. I feel a smirk coming on—just sayin'.

FAN PRICING

If you would like to find out what LMBPN is doing and the books we will be publishing, just sign up at http://lmbpn.com/email/. When you sign up, we notify you of books coming out for the week, any new posts of interest in the books and pop culture arena, and the fan pricing on Saturday.

Ad Aeternitatem,

Michael Anderle

## OTHER REVELATION OF ORICERAN UNIVERSE BOOKS

**The Unbelievable Mr. Brownstone**

*** Michael Anderle ***

Feared by Hell (1) - Rejected by Heaven (2) - Eye For An Eye (3) - Bring the Pain (4) - She is the Widow Maker (5) - When Angels Cry (6) - Fire with Fire (7) - Hail To The King (8) - Alison Brownstone (9) - One Bad Decision (10) - Fatal Mistake (11) - Karma Is A Bitch (12) - Vax Humana (13)

**I Fear No Evil**

*** Martha Carr and Michael Anderle ***

Kill the Willing (1) - Bury the Past, But Shoot it First (2) - Reload Faster (3) - Dead In Plain sight (4) - Tomb Raiding PHD (5) - Tomb Raider Emeritus (6)

**School of Necessary Magic**

*** Judith Berens ***

Dark Is Her Nature (1) - Bright Is Her Sight (2) - Wary Is Her Love (3) - Strong Is Her Hope (4) - Wicked Is Her Smile (5) - Strange Is Her Life (6) - Determined Is Her Path (7) - Epic Is Her Future (8)

**Rewriting Justice**

*** Martha Carr and Michael Anderle ***

Justice Served Cold (1) - Vengeance Served Hot (2) - Bounty Hunter Inc (03) - Beware The Hunter (4)

**The Daniel Chronicles**

The Artifact Enigma (1) - Artifact of the Sky Gods (2)

**The Leira Chronicles**

*** Martha Carr and Michael Anderle ***

Waking Magic (1) - Release of Magic (2) - Protection of Magic (3) - Rule of Magic (4) - Dealing in Magic (5) - Theft of Magic (6) - Enemies of Magic (7) - Guardians of Magic (8)

**The Soul Stone Mage Series**

*** Sarah Noffke and Martha Carr ***

House of Enchanted (1) - The Dark Forest (2) - Mountain of Truth (3) - Land of Terran (4) - New Egypt (5) - Lancothy (6) - Virgo (7)

**The Kacy Chronicles**

*** A.L. Knorr and Martha Carr ***

Descendant (1) - Ascendant (2) - Combatant (3) - Transcendent (4)

**The Midwest Magic Chronicles**

*** Flint Maxwell and Martha Carr***

The Midwest Witch (1) - The Midwest Wanderer (2) - The Midwest Whisperer (3) - The Midwest War (4)

**The Fairhaven Chronicles**

*** with S.M. Boyce ***

Glow (1) - Shimmer (2) - Ember (3) - Nightfall (4)

## BOOKS BY MICHAEL ANDERLE

For a complete list of books by Michael Anderle, please visit

**www.lmbpn.com/ma-books/**

All LMBPN Audiobooks are Available at Audible.com and iTunes. For a complete list of audiobooks visit:

**www.lmbpn.com/audible**

# CONNECT WITH MICHAEL ANDERLE

**Michael Anderle Social**

**Website:**
**http://kurtherianbooks.com/**

**Email List:**
**http://kurtherianbooks.com/email-list/**

**Facebook Here:**
https://www.facebook.com/OriceranUniverse/
https://www.
facebook.com/TheKurtherianGambitBooks/

www.ingramcontent.com/pod-product-compliance
Lightning Source LLC
Chambersburg PA
CBHW050241110726
47898CB00007B/2228

* 9 7 8 1 6 4 2 0 2 2 2 1 6 *